Armed & Marvelous

by
Pam Crooks

BOOK 8

ARMED & MARVELOUS
Copyright © 2023 Pam Crooks

Cover Design © Shanna Hatfield,
www.shannahatfield.com

Edited by: Linda Carroll-Bradd of Lustre Editing,
www.lustreediting.com

Excerpt: Lucky Shot (Pink Pistol Sisterhood Series) by Shanna Hatfield
Copyright © 2023 Shanna Hatfield

This book is licensed for your personal enjoyment only. All rights reserved, including the right to reproduce or transmit this book, or a portion thereof, in any form or by any means, electronic or mechanical, without permission in writing from the author, except for the use of brief quotations in a book review. This ebook may not be resold or uploaded for distribution to others.

ARMED & MARVELOUS is a work of fiction. Names, characters, places, brands, media and incidents are either the product of the author's imagination or are used fictitiously. The author acknowledges the trademarked status and trademark owners of various products referenced in this work of fiction, which have been used without permission. The publication/use of these trademarks is not authorized, associated with, or sponsored by, the trademark owners.

Version 2023.06
38,890 words.

:

Prologue

Uyak Bay, Kodiak Island, Alaska
May 10, 1955

If there was anything more exhilarating for Rexanna Brennan than wild game hunting in Wyoming or an exotic safari in Africa, it was bear hunting in Alaska. On a luxury yacht, no less. With her redbone coonhound, Mack, snoozing at her feet, and her trusted friend and fellow guide, Damien LeNoir, to assist, and, well, a hunting expedition didn't get much better than that.

But this was the thirteenth day of their trip.

Tomorrow, they'd have to pack up, disembark the St. Brendan, and return to California. Two days after that, Rexanna would start all over again with a new group of clients in a whole new location, as eager to shoot wild game as her current clients—wealthy airline executive, Stuart Langford, and his wife, Patrice, from Los Angeles.

Rexanna needed to find one more bear. Just one that their college-age daughter, Annie, who had accompanied them, could claim as a trophy. For her, for everyone, then the expedition would be a success.

Seated in her folding chair next to the main deck's wood-burning stove, Rexanna lifted the binoculars again to scan the forested mountains of Kodiak Island. As the owner of her own outfitting company, she understood the need for patience in scouting for game. Cruising the shoreline of the bay—with its breathtaking vistas—would be relaxing on any other day, but time was ticking.

Then, in a blink, something moved among the trees. A dark shape little more than a blob this far off the beach. Had she imagined it?

"Coffee, Rexanna?"

She ignored Damien. The more she stared through the lenses, though, the more convinced she became she'd mistaken the dark shape. Probably just wishful thinking, and more likely a shadow among countless others on those hills. The sun, the beautiful blue sky, the clouds, all combined to play tricks on her hopes to find Annie her Alaskan Kodiak bear. Whatever Rexanna saw, it was gone, and she lowered the binoculars.

Damien held out a porcelain mug, steaming from

strong coffee, sweetened with sugar and cream. Smiling her thanks, she took the mug and sipped. The warm liquid, just shy of hot, caressed her throat going down.

"St. Brendan is ignoring us today, eh?" Damien said in his faint French accent, crinkling his dark eyes over the beach and hills and searching, too.

Rexanna set her binoculars in her lap and curled her fingers around the mug. "St. Brendan is the patron saint of boatmen. St. Hubert is the guy we need right now."

Damien grinned. "Ah. The patron saint of hunters. We could use his help today, yes."

Rexanna sobered. "It'll be dusk in a few hours."

"Then too dark to hunt. She will be disappointed."

In somber unison, their gazes slid toward the young woman, seated on a vinyl-covered bench with her pants-clad legs tucked under her, a magazine in one hand. With her stylish pixie haircut, brown tweed hunting jacket, and pricey boots, Annie Langford reflected the affluent upbringing her parents gave her. She was a decent hunter with enough experience to want bragging rights and the proof of a bearskin rug to show off to her friends.

Rexanna understood what being twenty-one meant. She was only six years older, but she'd made her own way in the world without parents to pave her road. Counting pennies and earning her stripes in the hunting world garnered her a stellar reputation. Pride in her outfitting company produced plenty of sympathy for the young woman. What guide and outfitter wouldn't want the perfect hunting experience for their clients?

Perfection led to success, and Rexanna wasn't giving up on that bear just yet.

"Keep watch, will you?" she asked Damien, handing him the binoculars. "I'm going to talk to Annie for a minute." She leaned down to scratch Mack behind his floppy, rusty-red colored ears, then she rose and stepped around him to approach Annie. Stuart and Patrice, wearing matching wool buffalo-checked jackets, leaned their chubby bodies against the yacht's railing and marveled at the scenery. Both were tolerant of their daughter's need to shoot a bear; but then, they'd both shot their own and had the bearskins to prove it. For them, the pressure was off.

"Mind if I join you?" Rexanna asked, easing onto the cushion before the young woman even looked up from her reading.

"Nothing else to do, is there?" Annie sounded petulant, but she swung her legs to the deck floor, giving Rexanna more room.

"The day isn't over yet. We're not giving up." She gestured toward Damien, surveilling the hills with a skill honed over the years. "If there's a bear, we'll see him and hustle ourselves right off the boat. This is the time of year they come out to feed. They're out there."

"I know." She angled her head toward the lush, green mountain. A slight forty-something-degree breeze ruffled her wispy bangs.

Her disappointment pulled at Rexanna. If she could produce a ten-foot brown bear out of thin air and give Annie the thrill of the shot, she would in a heartbeat.

"What are you reading?" Hoping to keep her from dwelling on her disappointment, Rexanna indicated the magazine.

Annie closed the pages to reveal the cover and the red logo for the popular entertainment magazine, *Film*

Star Scoop. "Oh, just some article about Roan Bertoletti. Ever hear of him?"

"Sure." Rexanna nodded with a small shrug. She didn't often have time to go to the movies, but Roan had a face most women couldn't forget. "What about him?"

"Well, he was having an affair with Doreen Adams. You know, one of the actresses in his latest Western? She says, when she wanted to break up the relationship to save her marriage, he got mad and pushed her down the stairs."

"Really?" Rexanna's eyes widened.

"Really. Here's proof." Annie opened the magazine again, found the page she was looking for, and thrust it at Rexanna. "The article with a photo of her injuries."

Rexanna gaped at the black-and-white image of the young actress with her beauty marred by a swollen eye and puffy lip. "That's terrible."

"I feel so sorry for her. The rat."

"Well." Rexanna straightened with a disgusted cluck of her tongue. "I'm done with him and his movies. He doesn't deserve my time or money."

"Mine, either." Annie closed the magazine and tossed it aside, turning her pleading expression full force onto Rexanna. "Can we at least go ashore and scout the hills? Just because we can't see any Kodiaks from here doesn't mean they aren't around."

There they were. Back to the bears, and Rexanna couldn't blame Annie for persisting. Rexanna had been much the same when she was Annie's age—impatient to experience the most life could offer. When again would she get a chance to go on an Alaskan hunting expedition, with or without her parents? Rexanna smiled and stood. "Of course. Why not? Let's go break some sticks, shall we?"

Annie brightened at the suggestion, used by hunters to make some noise in hopes of spooking game into the open. She stood, too. "Oh, hurry, Rexanna! It won't take me long to get ready."

"I'll just grab my coat and hat from my cabin. Don't forget your rifle, and make sure you're dressed warm enough."

But Annie was already headed to the bench where a pile of guns were kept, sheathed in their carrying cases. Rexanna strode across the main deck, pausing only long enough to let Damien know the plan and to take her binoculars back. She kept her stride swift as she entered the galley and left her coffee mug in the sink, then kept going through the saloon to her cabin at the back.

Briskly, she donned her hunting coat and billed cap, then unsheathed her custom .416 Rigby big game rifle, strapping it over her shoulder. Dropping her binoculars into a roomy front pocket, Rexanna headed out of the cabin and met Damien rushing through the saloon.

"She left already. Better hurry, Rexanna."

Her step faltered. "Annie left? By herself?"

His mouth thinned. "She took Mack with her."

Rexanna's teeth clenched. It was bad enough Annie disobeyed Rexanna's orders to wait, but to leave the St. Brendan unaccompanied and to take Mack was enough to warrant some strong scolding.

Her dog had a lot of spirit and speed, and once he caught scent of game, big or small, he'd be off on his own on the mountain. Annie would never be able to stop him. A tendril of fear, of simmering anger, burned through Rexanna's chest, and she broke into a sprint toward the deck.

"Where were Stuart and Patrice? They just let her go?" she grated.

"They told her to wait for you, but once they lowered the boat and she climbed in, she just took off." His booted steps clamored behind her. "Sorry, Rexanna. Wish I could go, too."

"Just help me with the boat. I can't let her climb that mountain by herself."

Damien's responsibility lay with manning the yacht and staying with Annie's parents, both looking concerned by their daughter's disobedience. They worked quickly to lower the outboard into the frigid water.

"I'll come with you," Stuart said.

"No." Rexanna spoke sharply. The past thirteen days convinced her he would only slow her down, his age and lack of athleticism more of a detriment on a mountain than help. "She's not far ahead. I'll catch up with her." She settled on the wooden seat. "We'll be back soon."

With the motor revving, she took off, guiding the boat into a wide turn at high speed. They weren't so far off the shore that she couldn't see Annie pull up on the rocky beach and cut the power. Energized by the prospect of a hunt, Mack jumped out, ignoring Annie's call to come back.

Seeing her prized hunting dog lope up the mountain and disappear into the tree line only tightened Rexanna's belly with more worry. By the time she reached the beach and hopped out, Annie had disappeared, too.

Annie's determination to brag about her hunting prowess to her friends and her headstrong selfishness compelled her to ignore every rule Rexanna and Damien instilled in her and her parents the past thirteen days. Her bravado had completely overtaken her common sense. If Rexanna couldn't get to her soon enough....

Rexanna took precious moments to pull her binoculars from the jacket pocket to survey the mountain. Her ears pricked to the baying sound of Mack's barking, and then the lenses found Annie, stepping into a small clearing. In the shadows, her rifle in one hand, she waved at Rexanna with the other. She pointed into the trees, a sign of the direction she intended. Obviously, Annie had seen something, maybe the bear she wanted so desperately, and she was heading into the same area where Mack was.

If an animal was close enough to incite barking from Mack, then he'd be close to Annie, too. Gripping her .416, Rexanna hurried up the hill with her boots clomping over sand and gravel left behind from age-old glaciers. The higher she climbed, the cooler the air got, and it occurred to her, oddly, that Annie hadn't even taken the time to grab her coat.

A shot cracked through the mountain, then another, and Rexanna froze in mid-step. The sounds were close, and her brain strove to discern the precise direction, even as a horrible fear burst through her veins that Annie might have made a mistake. A terrible, frightening, *amateur* mistake, of shooting uphill and not down....

Then, the roar, filled with rage and blood-curdling ferocity, shook the mountain and chilled Rexanna to her bones. Lifting the .416 to her shoulder, she treaded stealthily over the rough terrain, around the trees, snapping twigs and pine needles, her ears peeled to the lumbering footsteps she could hear and not quite place. She had no fear for her own safety, only that of a young woman, and of Mack, too. If Rexanna could do anything, if she'd gained any skill at all during her years of hunting, she had to get to the bear before he got to Annie.

And then, there he was, crimson staining his chest. Teeth bared, eyes glittering, his growl terrifying. Ten feet tall, if he was an inch. One thousand pounds, easy. Trophy worthy. Focused on the young woman he intended as revenge.

Annie stood silent, mouth agape, paralyzed in shock. Rexanna shouted to take another shot to save herself, to run, if nothing else, but she did nothing, *nothing,* and Rexanna braced the .416 against her shoulder....

Hampered by the tangle of trees and branches, she needed precious time to sight the bear in her scope and pull the trigger. Every second counted. She couldn't miss. Annie's life depended on it. Mack's, too. Barely feeling the rifle's kick, she shot again and again, but the crazed bear, still powerful, lunged for the terrified young woman, the adrenaline firing through him like bullets out of the Rigby's barrel. His mammoth arm swung outward in one savage swipe and flung her through the air like a wet rag. His claws tore her clothes and skin and splattered blood.

Rexanna shot again. Only then did the bear

succumb, falling hard on top of Annie, dulling her scream under his roar... until the terrible sounds ended, and the mountain fell silent.

1

Wallace, Kansas
May 20, 1955

One week. Two funerals.

Rexanna stood graveside in the Wallace Cemetery, arm in arm with her beloved Grandma Harrie, and stared at the gleaming wooden casket already lowered into the ground. Aunt Trixie had died unexpectedly from a cancer that spread throughout her body but blessedly spared her of pain. If she was aware of her illness, she told no one. If she wasn't aware, it was because she never trusted doctors and wouldn't have sought their treatment, which only meant her loss was a shock to everyone.

Reclusive and crazy as a loon, her aunt was as gentle as a kitten, as perplexing as a puzzle, and as different from Rexanna as two women could be. The three years Rexanna had lived with her after her parents' deaths from an automobile accident hadn't been easy. Still, losing her aunt just about ripped Rexanna's heart out.

What was left after losing Annie, that is.

Rexanna steeled herself against showing emotion. From feeling it. She had no more tears to shed, but the sting in her eyes taunted the thought. The awful weight of her failures kept her back straight, her shoulders squared, and her body rigid. If she let go of her grandmother, she'd likely crumple.

The priest closed his missal and invited the Brennan family and friends to eulogize Aunt Trixie. No one did. Least of all, Rexanna, who owed her a wealth of gratitude for the time they'd lived together and for having the semblance of family she'd lost from her parents' death.

The words weren't in her heart. And that was a failure, too.

Finally, Grandma Harrie stepped forward, gently bringing Rexanna with her, and dropped a rose onto the casket. Rexanna did the same. The action required little thought and even less emotion. That would come later, she hoped. Aunt Trixie deserved at least that.

The warm Kansas wind fluttered the canvas canopy

over their heads and tugged at the wide brim on Rexanna's black hat. It seemed hauntingly final, seeing the rose in that hole. On top of the simple casket. So low in the ground the breeze couldn't reach the petals. Deprived of life, their beauty would soon shrivel, abandoned in the dark. Gone forever, like Aunt Trixie.

Fighting the sadness her morbid thoughts wrought, Rexanna moved back toward the row of chairs the morticians had set up. Her grandmother patted Rexanna's hand, settled in the crook of her arm, clad in black, too.

"You'll stay for the luncheon, won't you, honey?" she asked.

Rexanna hesitated. The funeral-goers came out of respect for her grandparents, who had lived on the T Bar M Ranch their entire married lives. Aunt Trixie was their son's sister-in-law. Before they were killed, Gil and Muriel, Rexanna's parents, had lived on the T Bar M Ranch, too, and watched over Trixie whenever she needed watching. Which was pretty much her whole crazy, spinster life.

After burying their son and daughter-in-law, her grandparents took over the task of Aunt Trixie's care. In a small, quiet town like Wallace, everyone knew everyone else. They knew Trixie. Naturally, they knew Rexanna, too.

But she was in no mood for any kind of a reunion that included small talk and civility. The effort to decipher faces and names, to feign friendliness after being gone so many years, after what happened to Annie, was too much.

"I'm not hungry, Grandma," she said finally. "I'll just go to the house and take a nap, if you don't mind."

"You need to eat," her grandmother said. "You didn't take the time to have a decent breakfast when you drove out to the ranch."

"After driving most of the night, I needed a shower more."

Her eyes the color of fine leather, Grandma Harrie's shrewd gaze lingered moments too long, and Rexanna fought the urge to squirm. She knew what her grandmother was thinking. That the explanation Rexanna gave about the horrible way Annie died was minimal, at best, and made over the phone at the same time she'd been informed about Aunt Trixie's death.

So much loss. So much grief.

Rexanna had driven from California to Kansas, from one funeral to another. She needed a little more time to work through the unfairness of all that she'd lost.

From all that had gone wrong.

Her biggest failure, most of all.

It was only natural that her grandmother would have questions. But Rexanna wasn't yet ready to give answers.

"All right, honey." Grandma Harrie nodded, her expression softening. "You'll feel much better after you get some rest. We won't be in town but for a few hours, and you'll have supper with us, for sure. We need to talk. Decisions need to be made."

"What kind of decisions?"

"Decisions that can wait." The deep voice swiveled her attention to her grandfather. Tall, broad-shouldered, with silver threaded through his dark hair, his smoky gray eyes warmed over her beneath the brim of his Stetson. "You're not going anywhere for a spell, young lady."

His long arm slid around her shoulders and pulled her against his chest. Her heart swelled. For the first time in a long time, she felt unequivocally loved. Unjudged. Protected, most of all.

"I'm not?" she asked.

"Why not send her out to Trixie's place, Harrie?" he asked over Rexanna's black-hatted head. "It's hers now, anyway, and she might as well start getting used to it." He grinned down at her, giving her a charming wink, convincing her more than ever that, even in his seventies, Cord Brennan was the handsomest rancher around.

"Oh-oh." Rexanna sighed. "I'm not sure I like the sound of that."

"She's just come home, Cord. I want her with us."

"She won't be that far away. An easy drive."

"It's silly for her to be at Trixie's when we have plenty of room. I want to *see* her." Her grandmother's mouth curved downward. "The place needs work, Cord. You know it does. Rexanna needs a better welcome than what Trixie's cabin could give her."

"Let her decide, then." His gaze returned to Rexanna, but less teasing this time. "Some folks need to be alone to work out their troubles. Others need the strength that comes from being with family to get them through it." He gave her shoulders a firm squeeze. "What'll it be for you, Rexi?"

Her throat swelled from the easy use of her childhood nickname. No one called her Rexi anymore, and hearing it now moved something in her chest.

It'd been too long.

Why hadn't she come back more often?

She drew in a breath and let it out again. Maybe her grandfather was right. Maybe returning to the home her aunt had given her was what she needed to do. Just for a little while. The cabin hadn't always been a happy place for her, but it was more home than her grandparents' big house. If she needed to change her mind, Grandma Harrie would accommodate her every wish.

Besides, Rexanna wasn't staying in Kansas. She'd be here only long enough to get her feet back on solid ground again. Her head on straight.

Her outfitting business—her clients—needed her.

And she needed them.

Thank goodness for Damien. By the time he returned from the current hunting expedition in Tanzania, East Africa, Rexanna would be ready to get back to work.

"I'll stay at the cabin." Her scrutiny slid over the small group of people chatting among themselves, paying her no mind, while others meandered back to their cars to drive to the church hall for lunch. Uncle Charlie, Grandma Harrie's younger brother, whom she'd always credited as being the Cupid who helped her fall in love with Grandpa, was among them, his wife at his side. Grandma's younger sister, Adelaide, was the only family member not in attendance, due to her commitments in California, her employment with a hot-shot movie producer, of all things, at the top of the list. "Just like old times, right?"

"Well..." Grandpa hesitated, but there was a definite twinkle in his eyes. "I'll let you decide. You might be inclined to change your thinking."

"*Not* like old times?" Her brow arched.

"Nope."

"You're scaring me, Grandpa."

He chuckled outright and chucked her under the chin. "Just be open-minded, okay? Your Aunt Trixie was always full of surprises."

"I'll drive out with her." Grandma reached for her black purse on the chair seat, giving Rexanna no chance to speculate on what *surprises* meant. "I'll be back as soon as I can."

"Grandma. I know the way out to Aunt Trixie's," she insisted. "Your place is here, with your friends and Uncle Charlie."

Rexanna's attention took in the dispersing funeral-goers and landed on a late-model, plum-colored Chrysler sedan that seemed as out of place on the Kansas prairie as an antelope in a chicken coop. The man who opened the driver's side door did, too, with the cut of his dark suit coat superb over his shoulders. The fabric was of a deep blue color that boasted a faint sheen under the sun and cried out *expensive*. No rancher she knew would dress that fancy. But then, she'd been gone a long time. How did she know how ranchers dressed these days?

Well, she didn't have the time to give him another thought. She'd likely never see him again, and she refocused on her grandmother with clearer thoughts.

"My place is with you, honey. I just want to make sure you're settled in."

"But, Grandma."

"She's not going to change her mind, Rexi. Might as well humor her." Her grandfather dipped under her hat brim to place a quick kiss on her cheek. "Come over for supper. The Altar Society ladies will send us home with leftovers from lunch. We'll have plenty, and Grandma won't have to cook."

Rexanna made no promises, but her hug gave the impression she would do as he asked. Alongside Grandma Harrie, she left the funeral home's canopy and walked on tiptoe to keep her heels from sinking into the soft ground. Her grandmother headed toward her older model Pontiac, parked in front of Rexanna's even older Ford F1 pickup, painted in a subtle copper tone hue.

Mack waited on the driver's seat, his rusty-red head halfway out the window, his tongue hanging out one side of his mouth. He kept as close an eye on her as he would a prairie dog in its hole, and she ruffled his head in greeting, nudging him away so she could take his place.

"I'll follow you, Grandma," she said out the window, tugging her black skirt over her knees as she settled in behind the steering wheel.

Her grandmother's smile and agreeable wave meant she was pleased to have Rexanna compliant, even though she'd lost the argument about them both going to the luncheon. Rexanna used the key and the dashboard's push-button start, stepped on the clutch, tapped the accelerator, and the pickup truck revved. She drove into place behind Grandma Harrie on the narrow cemetery road and readied herself for what kind of craziness she'd find at Aunt Trixie's cabin.

It was worse than she thought.

The old cabin looked as forlorn as ever, with its paint chipped away down to bare wood. The green shingles on the roof needed replacing, the windows needed a good washing, and the dead flowers along the foundation should have been pulled out two seasons ago.

But it was the hanging *things* all along the front porch's exterior frame and ceiling that struck Rexanna as being just plain weird.

"We tried to fix it up for her," Grandma said quietly, approaching the pickup after a restrained closing of her car's door, as if she was reluctant to disturb the eerie silence. "She wouldn't let us touch anything."

"Why not?"

Grandma shrugged. "She just said she'd get around to it soon. But soon never came."

Rexanna slid out of the truck, and Mack followed with a graceful leap off the seat. She, too, closed the door with a gentle latch, her stare unwavering on the porch.

"They're like chandeliers, in an odd sort of way," she murmured.

"Yes. When the breeze is just right, they sway and catch the light. Some of them even tinkle and chime. I find myself mesmerized by them."

"She made these herself?" Rexanna asked, moving toward the steps.

"Every piece of wire, tin, glass, wood... everything hanging here she found and cut to fit the vision she had for them in her head."

Rexanna paused before climbing. "Why?"

"They made her happy."

"How?"

"I can't explain it. I'm no expert on troubled

minds, honey, but... well, I think they were her friends."

"Friends." She blinked in disbelief.

"These creations kept her company. They kept her busy and stimulated. They gave her a reason to get up every morning."

"Wow, Grandma."

"I know. It's odd."

"It's craziness to me." She climbed the pair of stairs and, reaching upward, tapped a finger on the closest hanging thing. The wire swayed to ting against the one next to it. Plastic beads hung with discarded cola bottle caps, providing an array of mismatched colors.

"She called them her little birdies." Her grandmother cocked her head, clearly attempting to hide her amusement and expecting Rexanna's disbelief.

Rexanna's expression didn't fail her. "Crazy *and* weird."

"Don't be so hard on her, Rexi. She was content in her own way." Holding the screen door open with her hip, Grandma produced a key ring from her purse, chose one, and slid it into the front door's lock.

"How did she see birdies out of wire and string?"

"Because they sway and dip in the wind, free and unburdened, and these creations sound pretty, too. If you look closely, every one of them has a feather in it. Somewhere."

Rexanna could only shake her head. "Well, birds do have feathers, I guess."

The door swung open, and Aunt Trixie's craziness faded against the prospect of stepping into Rexanna's former home. Despite the brightness of the day, closed curtains kept the main room dim. A faint mustiness hung in the air, and her slow sweep of the small cabin revealed nothing had changed. Same pictures on the wall, same lackluster furniture, same fake flowers on the fireplace mantel. Even the same magazines were stacked on the coffee table.

"It's like I never left," she breathed.

"She hoped you'd change your mind and come back, you know. She never gave up hope." Grandma Harrie gave a quick, sideways yank on the drapes covering the main window, and sunlight poured in. Mack moseyed into a bright swath and lay down. "I think, in her own way, she wanted to preserve the three years she had with you. Like some sort of time capsule."

A swift ball of emotion rose in Rexanna's throat. Guilt for having left? Or the rush of disappointment that her teen years had deprived her of the patience and ability to get along with her aunt, who never had a husband or children of her own, and who would've kept Rexanna in an unbreachable bubble if she could?

Her love, certainly, had been too stifling and unyielding for a young girl who only wanted to break free, see the world, and live her own life away from her family's ranch.

"Here's the cabin's key for you," Grandma Harrie said, setting it on the mantel next to a wooden box, the one thing Rexanna hadn't seen before. "Trixie had pretty much given up on housekeeping. She used to be so meticulous. The place needs a deep cleaning, but I straightened up as best I could after she died. It seemed only right to do that for her. Everything's been vacuumed and dusted, and I put fresh sheets on both beds. There're a few groceries in the cupboards, but

Trixie didn't cook much. Not like she used to." Grandma frowned. "In fact, I'm not even sure she bathed regularly toward the end."

Rexanna heaved a slow breath. If the cancer hadn't left her suffering, her own inner demons did.

"Do you want me to help you unload your truck?" Grandma asked.

"No. I can do it. I didn't bring much. Thank you, though."

"All right, honey. I'd best hurry." She dropped a gentle kiss on Rexanna's cheek. "Supper tonight. Don't forget."

"I won't." She'd go. It was the least she could do after all Grandma Harrie had done. "Drive carefully back to town."

Her grandmother smiled. "I've made that trip so many times, I can do it in my sleep." She pulled open the door, took a step out, then turned back. Sunlight glinted on her hair, once a vibrant cinnamon, but now mostly gray and upswept into a stylish bouffant. Her expression had grown serious. "We were the only family Trixie had left. We took care of her as much as we could. As much as she'd let us. In case you're wondering."

Rexanna's brows furrowed. "I wasn't wondering at all."

Why would she, when her life in Kansas all but faded away when she was in the exotic wilds on some continent, hunting game with clients who had the money to pay for the experience?

No, never once had she worried about Aunt Trixie.

Knowing what she knew now, hanging things and all, she should have.

"Someone always came out to check on her. Roan, mostly," Grandma added. "He was especially considerate of her."

Her attention snagged on the man's name. If he'd been kind to her aunt, Rexanna vowed to find a way to express her gratitude.

"Who is he, this Ron?" she asked. "One of the T Bar M cowboys?"

"Not Ron. Roan. R-O-A-N." Her eyes twinkled. "You know. Like the color of a horse? And yes, he works for us. Hired out not too long ago."

"Roan." Her memory twitched at the word.

"Surely, you've heard of him, Rexi. The actor from Hollywood. Roan Bertoletti."

2

Rexanna stood slack-jawed for long moments after Grandma Harrie rushed off with a promise to explain more later. By the time Rexanna shook off the shock, a full blast of contempt took over.

Roan Bertoletti? The Western movie actor who had had an affair with another man's wife? He'd pushed the actress down the stairs in a fit of rage and left her with terrible injuries. What in the world was he doing in Kansas? On the T Bar M, no less?

If he'd hurt Aunt Trixie, or taken advantage of her in her fragile mental state, somehow— Rexanna's chest burned—she'd smack the man herself.

If only Rexanna would've taken the time to read the *Film Star Scoop* article Annie had shown her, she'd have the full story, then.

Did her grandparents know what he'd done? If they didn't, he'd completely fooled everyone into thinking he was someone he wasn't.

Wasn't that what actors did? Deceive people? Play a part to draw them into their fantasy world?

Grandma Harrie had been quite enamored with him.

Oh, the man was good.

Rexanna huffed, yanked off her black heels, and strode into her old bedroom. What was it her grandmother had said? He was *especially considerate* of Aunt Trixie.

What did that mean?

Considerate. Really? How?

Supper tonight couldn't come fast enough. Her grandparents would get an earful, for sure. They deserved to know how wretched a man Roan Bertoletti really was.

The prospect of enlightening her family cooled some of the contempt burning inside her, reminding her she'd forgotten to unload her truck. Exasperated, she slid back into her heels and headed out to the porch. Mack barely gave her a cursory glance.

She unlatched the pickup's gate and pulled her suitcase out of the truck bed. Two more trips into the cabin followed with hunting rifles and boxes of cartridges. Once the Ford was fully unloaded, she locked the front door, returned to the pale-pink bedroom that had once been hers, and paused.

A time capsule, Grandma had said.

Memories entrapped her, a dizzying whoosh that threw her back to the time she'd spent within these walls. Shaken and moved, she eased onto the mattress, still too lumpy, still covered by the pink-and-yellow quilt her mother had made when Rexanna was three years old, having outgrown her crib and ready for a big-girl bed. The stitched squares had faded over the years and grown velvety soft from countless washings, and her eyes watered from unexpected emotion. Anyone else might have thrown away the threadbare covering. Not Aunt Trixie. Not Grandma, either. They'd saved and preserved a small piece of her childhood for Rexanna, no doubt hoping maturity would bring with it deep appreciation for their efforts.

It worked. Her appreciation reached in deep and squeezed her heart, leaving Rexanna more touched by their thoughtfulness than she could ever have expected.

There was the double-sized bed with its decades-old wrought-iron headboard, too. And the blonde dresser with her bride doll propped against the mirror. A poster of a rakishly handsome Frank Sinatra in a fedora hung on the wall, strategically placed so she could pretend his dreamy blue eyes were looking right at her while she fell asleep.

Rexanna's head moved in sheepish amusement. In the years since, she'd traded her innocent, sheltered life for adventure and travel. No more girlish bedrooms, but tents and lodges and an occasional luxury yacht. No cattle and horses, anymore, but exotic wild game, the likes of which had never set foot on Kansas soil before.

Sighing away her melancholy, she stood and lifted the hem of her black dress and slip to unclasp the hooks on her girdle, releasing the nylons they held in place. Careful not to snag them, she eased the gossamer stockings off her legs and laid them in a neat fold on the dresser. Her girdle and wide-brimmed hat claimed more space, and after removing her dress, she hung it up in the closet with a few of Aunt Trixie's old clothes and shut the door.

She hoped never to wear that dress again.

She'd had to buy the entire outfit for Annie's funeral, since there was no time to return to her small rental in Montana. Not that she had any appropriate funeral attire there, anyway. New nylons, new girdle, new slip. Matching hat and heels. Never once realizing she'd have to don them all again after Aunt Trixie's passing.

She pulled back the old quilt and, wearing only her slip and underwear, she climbed between the sheets, crisp and clean and smelling of the wind.

Grandma had done that for her, too.

Warmed and comforted, Rexanna closed her eyes and slept.

A baying howl jerked her awake. Two more, in quick succession, and she sat bolt upright. Heart pounding, her brain a fog of confusion, she wrestled with the uncertainty of where she was and why.

A knock rapped against the door, and Mack howled again. Her brain cleared. Rexanna flung back the quilt and leapt off the bed. Someone was here, at Aunt Trixie's cabin. What time was it? Who would come all the way out here? Grandma? Grandpa? Why?

The mirror jolted her with the image of her in her

slip, blonde hair falling over her right eye like it always did when she didn't use a barrette. Her dishabille and sleep-mussed hair elicited a yelp of dismay. She hadn't even opened her suitcase yet. Where was a robe? Did Aunt Trixie have something she could wear?

She yanked open the closet door, riffled through her aunt's clothes, and found a red-and-white striped housedress. One corner of the pocket was torn, and a small stain leapt off the bodice like a beacon, but she threw it on, worked the top-to-bottom buttons together, belted the thing around her waist, and hurried out of the bedroom.

In the main room, she snuck a peek out the window with a discreet lifting of the edge of the drapery her grandmother had parted. A plum-colored sedan sat in the drive, evoking an image of the man at the cemetery who had climbed into the driver's seat, and she sucked in a breath of surprise.

Why would he come out here to see her?

He knocked again. Mack stood with his body alert, his tail wagging. His brown eyes appealed up at her, as if to say, '*Hurry up and open the door, will you?*'.

Rexanna threaded her fingers through her hair and off her face. She drew in a calming breath, turned the lock, and opened the door.

He still wore that classy suit from the funeral, the color a darker blue now that he stood on her porch, out of the sun. He'd removed the tie and loosened the shirt's top button. He had a nice neck, tanned and lean, with a sprinkling of dark hairs to tease he had plenty more on his chest.

"Rexanna?"

He had a nice voice, too. Deep and pleasant. Polite

and respectful, and how could she think all that about him from only one spoken word?

Still, her observance of him, the way he affected her by noticing every detail about him, wouldn't end. Like how he had beautiful eyes, thick-lashed, as dark as a raven's feathers, as dark as his hair, swept back in the popular pompadour style. He had a foreign look about him, as if he'd been Mediterranean born and bred, and had she known any man more handsome?

He left her tongue-tied and rattled. Little wonder, since his gaze drifted over her, his mouth in a faint curve, as if seeing her with mussed hair and wearing the old housedress amused him. As if she wasn't the only female to have been affected by him like this...

Her back stiffened. She'd faced down moose and mountain lions and wild boar plenty of times. She could face down one man on her porch, even if he was spit-polished to perfection. And she wasn't.

She had good reason not to be, and his amusement at her expense stung. She refused to fall into the same camp as any number of women who no doubt swooned all over him and his handsomeness with no regard for their own pride and dignity.

Rexanna hung on to hers and refused to let go.

"Yes," she said. "Rexanna Brennan."

He nodded. Once. Likely, he knew her full name already, since he'd driven all the way out here to see her.

"And you are?" she demanded, making herself sound haughtier than she normally would, adding a dramatic lift to her brow for emphasis.

"Name's Roan."

Her heart rate hiccupped. "Roan?"

"Bertoletti."

"Roan Bertoletti." Recognition jolted through her like the twang of a bowstring. Her brain emptied. Until it filled up again with an image of that poor, injured actress.

"Harrie asked me to check on you," he said.

Her eyes narrowed in grave suspicion. "Why would she do that?"

"Because it's getting late."

That threw her. Supper at her grandparents'. She sucked in a little breath of panic. "It is? What time is it?"

"Just after four."

She'd slept longer than she intended. Grandma Harrie hadn't given her a time, but by the shadows on the porch, Rexanna would have to leave soon.

"She's looking forward to supper with you," he added.

"I suppose you even know what we're having."

"Leftovers from the luncheon." His raven eyes crinkled. "The women around here are great cooks. None better than Harrie, though."

Rexanna clamped her teeth. She'd cooked for him? Why did her grandmother have to be so chatty with this man? Telling him her business, right along with Rexanna's, allowing them to be on a first-name basis, like they were lifelong friends, or something?

Which they weren't.

Roan Bertoletti and his crackerjack California acting career was as different from Grandma's life on the ranch as black was from white, and once she found out the person he really was, well, she'd be sorely disappointed she'd fallen for his charm.

Mack bayed, wagged his tail non-stop, and Roan squatted to give him some affectionate head and ear rubs.

"Nice-looking dog. What's his name?"

"Mack. He's a coonhound."

"Bet he's good on the trail."

"Better than good. None better."

Roan stood again, and from the way Mack stared up at him like a lovestruck pup, he'd won over one more member of her family.

"Heard you were a hunter," he said, his voice low. Impressed, maybe.

"Yep. Big game."

"Heard that, too."

"What else do you know about me, Mr. Bertoletti?"

His mouth quirked. "Not enough to keep your hackles up, that's for sure."

"My hackles are just fine." It was a bit of a fib, but she felt better for clarifying.

"I know you've been gone a long time, and there're a few things around here you need to know."

Her hackles didn't settle much. It'd be easy to read more into his comment, given his sordid past, but no doubt he meant something different. "Like what?"

"Another reason why I came by. To show you."

She banked her surprise. "It's not necessary to show me anything. I used to live out here. Besides, my grandparents will be a good resource for that information, don't you think?"

"They were the ones who asked."

Curiosity, in spite of everything, flickered and bloomed. "Oh?"

"Would you like to change into something... more appropriate, Rexanna?" he asked with a cool lift to his brow.

She hated how he sounded so superior and practical. Even if he didn't mean to, she *felt* like he did, and what did it matter to him how she was dressed?

She just wanted him off her porch.

Still, her gaze dropped involuntarily to find that her hurried buttoning was one button-closing off, leaving the housedress's hem lopsided and the lace on her slip showing. Barelegged, barefoot, and with the dress hanging haphazardly from its faulty fastening, well, no wonder he sounded so sanctimonious.

In a spurt of self-conscious rebellion, she stood a little taller, yanked her skirt downward past the edge of her slip, and crossed her arms over her chest. So what if he could see a little lace? It wouldn't be the first time he saw a woman's intimates, if the stories about him were true.

"I don't have time." If he thought she was climbing into his purple Chrysler with him, he had another think coming. She was only accompanying him because her grandparents wanted her to. "Where are we going, anyway?"

"Just a short walk." Inclining his head to avoid one of Aunt Trixie's hanging things, he descended one step. "I'll wait, if you want to put on shoes."

"Don't need shoes."

"Up to you." On the ground, he extended his arm, offering her a hand, as if being barefoot made her incapable of walking down the steps on her own. "Just stay to the grass, if you can."

She ignored his mannerly offer, and his arm

lowered. There wasn't much of a lawn, and what little there was needed mowing, but the grass cushioned her feet, at least. Though she made sure to keep distance between them, her awareness turned acute, like it did when she sensed game hiding in brush. The top of her head barely reached his chin, but he had the advantage of wearing shoes, the leather of which looked as expensive as his suit.

He kept his stride easy and slow to match hers. Their walking would have been pleasurable, if she'd been of a mind to enjoy it. If he was a different person, especially. But it'd been so long since she'd been this way, beyond Aunt Trixie's cabin, that she kept staring at the peeling paint and yardwork which needed to be done.

"This place is a mess," she said quietly.

"It wasn't to Trixie."

Her head swiveled toward him. "She couldn't see it?"

"If she could, she didn't care."

Rexanna sighed. "She never used to be careless."

"She wasn't the same person you knew."

He made her feel like she was the outsider, instead of the other way around. Rexanna halted with a scowl. "What makes you the expert on the kind of person she was? She was my aunt my whole life, and you... how long have you been working on the T Bar M, anyway?"

"Long enough to see her decline. She went downhill fast."

"Oh, no." Rexanna's stomach sank. "Why?"

"Let's keep going. I'll show you why." His lean fingers grasped her elbow, guiding her forward, and she didn't think to resist. Until she remembered what he'd done in California, that is, and she pulled her arm free, taking a couple of steps sideways for good measure.

His mouth thinned, but he kept his stride steady, staying on the grass out of consideration for her bare feet and avoiding a gravel road leading to the barn with a nice-sized corral attached. After her parents' deaths, Rexanna had kept her palomino mare in that corral. Then the year came when Rexanna left the ranch, and since Aunt Trixie was scared to death of horses, her grandparents sold the mare to a family with a house full of kids. It was the only reason Rexanna gave her permission to sell, as much as it just about ripped her heart out. Those kids were home every day to give her horse love and care.

Rexanna wasn't. And couldn't.

Metal fencing had been added to the rails, enclosing the area securely to keep predators out. The corral was empty; whatever T Bar M stock the fencing kept in was nowhere around.

Roan halted and slid a sharp whistle between his teeth. Through the open barn doors, a furry head and long neck appeared. Two more woolly animals, each different than the others, joined him, a sight Rexanna never expected to see on her family's cattle ranch.

She gasped in wide-eyed surprise. "Alpacas?"

Not surprising she knew what they were. Alpacas, not llamas. Animals were her livelihood, but Roan hadn't a clue about either when he first arrived on the T Bar M five months ago. Cord and Rexanna's Uncle Charlie weren't experts, either, but they shared what they knew with him out of necessity. A few books from the library and hours of studying helped, too. In the end, it was the time Roan spent with them every day that made taking care of them a real pleasure.

The trio with their distinctive, colorful wool trotted to the corral fence to greet him and check out Rexanna.

One white, one mostly black with some gray thrown in, and the other a pale brown, like coffee with too much cream. Their round eyes shone with unabashed curiosity about her, and crooning greetings for each of them, she reached over the fence to pet their woolly necks.

"They're cute," she said.

"Friendly, too."

"What compelled my grandfather to raise alpacas? He's all about cattle, not sheep. What changed?"

"Trixie did."

Rexanna didn't seem to notice Mack with his nose to the ground, sniffing up one side of the corral fence and down another. She must trust her dog wouldn't run off. The ranch was a big place. Thousands of acres, and all that open space left Roan uneasy. Made for a hound's paradise. If Mack took off, no telling how far he'd go or if they'd ever be able to catch him.

"I don't understand." Rexanna turned back toward him. "As far as I know, Aunt Trixie never even owned a goldfish. How does she figure into raising alpacas?"

In her puzzlement, Rexanna tilted her head. Some of her blonde hair fell forward onto her forehead, over her eye, catching enough sunlight to make him notice. Made him think about how pretty her hair was. How smooth it'd feel if he ran his fingers through it.

She was a beaut, for sure. Slender, athletically fit, with reddish-brown eyes and a natural confidence he didn't often see from the superficial, ridiculously vain women he'd known in California. Whenever her family spoke of her, they spoke with pride about her courage and accomplishments. The responsibility of owning her own business, especially—hunting wild game of all things—in a man's world.

Roan pulled his thoughts into a different direction. The answer she waited for, mostly, and he rested his forearm on the corral's top rail, only to remember the risk of snagging the sleeve of his suit coat, which cost more than anyone with good sense would pay. He removed his arm, hooking his thumb into his waistband instead.

"Your grandparents worried about her. Guess she got to where she wouldn't leave the cabin," he said. "Didn't associate with folks much. Wasn't good for her, being alone so much."

Rexanna didn't move. "Was it because of me? That I left?"

Roan didn't want her to feel the blame, but it was there. In the truth and in her heart.

"It wore on her, yeah."

She glanced away. "I never knew... she got that bad."

Roan's gut clenched. His own mother had suffered in much the same way. Difference was, he'd been with her to the end, had done everything he could, and it hadn't helped. "Nothing anyone could do about it."

She swept her hair behind her ear, a quick movement that might've meant she was frustrated. Or hurting.

"Harrie thought the alpacas might be a way to bring her out of her depression." He kept talking. Rexanna needed to know the story, all of it. Her being gone didn't mean she shouldn't. She'd been protected long enough, in his opinion. Understanding Trixie would remove some of the mystery about her for Rexanna. All the crazy things she said and did that folks didn't understand. In Rexanna's case, from what he'd heard, the resentment, too. Years worth of it. "Harrie hoped they'd give her something to do every day. Taking care of them and such."

"Aunt Trixie must have done a good job." Rexanna's voice softened. "They're healthy. Clean and happy, too."

Roan shrugged. That was because of him, but she'd figure it out eventually. The story wasn't finished yet.

"She did what she could, I guess. I wasn't around at that time, but she had help. Your grandparents, your uncle... they came out every day. There were four in the herd, then. Plenty for her to handle." He shrugged. "Maybe too many. Who knows?"

"Now there's three. Why would Grandpa sell one? Alpacas are social. They need each other to survive." Her gaze touched on each of them, bumping playfully against each other. "Or did one get sick or something?"

"A wolf got into the barn. Killed him. They think the alpaca fought to protect the rest of his herd from being attacked. At least, that's what Cord thought."

"Oh, no." She breathed the words in dismay. "What a shame."

"More than a shame, Rexanna. Just about did your aunt in."

Her expression clouded. "What do you mean?"

"She blamed herself. Wouldn't have anything more to do with them. Just ignored them, from what I hear."

"And she became even more of a recluse." Her comment, hushed and troubled, held more conviction than question.

"Worse than ever."

Rexanna turned toward the cabin's porch, then

back toward him. "No wonder she spent so much time on her... her hanging things."

"Can't kill those. They were all she had. Gave her some control and made her feel safe, I suppose."

"Poor Aunt Trixie."

She exhaled, the sound quivering and distressed. Roan hoped she wouldn't start to cry. Weeping females had always been his undoing.

"We added the metal fencing to the corral after the wolf attack, and he hasn't been around since. She got better, eventually," he said. Might be an exaggeration, but there was some truth in it, and he wanted Rexanna to feel better. "Her little birdies became her sole focus in life. They made her happy."

"That's what my grandmother said."

"It's true."

"She also said you took good care of her."

He shrugged. "I checked up on her. I wasn't the only one."

Her eyes narrowed, as if her thoughts were narrowed, too. Like in a tunnel. Focused on one thing. Made him want to look inside her brain and know what she was thinking.

He matched her stare, ignoring the grim tightening in his belly. The dreaded sense she knew more about him than she let on.

"Thank you for that," she said finally. "For taking care of her and the alpacas." They took her attention again, leaning over the top rail to nudge her shoulder, winning more of her petting. "Three males, right?"

"Right."

"Do they have names?"

"Trixie named them after the four seasons. Winter,

Spring, Summer, and Fall." He'd teased her once about her choices, but her explanation, he had to admit, made sense. "Can you figure out who's who?"

"Bet I can." Her expression lightened. "The white one is Winter. For snow. Let's see... the black one... for storms, I'll guess, so Summer. And the brown one must be... well, I'm going to say Fall. But he could be Spring, too."

"You were right the first time. He's Fall." His mouth curved. "Their names are Winter, Summer, and Fall. Good job, Rexanna."

Their gazes held for a moment, gifting him with the pleasure she'd derived from her guessing victories, warming him from it, but in the next, she sobered. Which took away Roan's pleasure, too. And chilled him.

There came that uneasy feeling again, making him think she was holding something back. Worrying him about what she didn't say.

"Are the alpacas yours now, Roan?" she asked quietly. "Did my grandfather give the herd to you, since you've been taking care of them all along?"

He frowned. "No. Why would he?"

"You seem to walk on water around here."

She wouldn't know how hard he'd worked to gain her family's acceptance. How humiliating it had been to try anything, say anything, to earn their trust. He credited his acting career for that, for winning them over at a time when he was likely the biggest outsider ever to set foot on T Bar M dirt.

Without the ranch, without the Brennans, he wouldn't have a home. A life worth respecting. A reputation.

Now, because of them, he could sleep at night.

"Think that if you want," he growled. "But I only brought you out here because this herd is yours now. Up to you to take care of them. I'll show—"

"Me?" Her jaw lagged. "I'm not staying."

"Everything Trixie had, she left to you. Common knowledge around here. Has been for a long time. That's how much you meant to her."

Rexanna's eyes instantly welled. Her breath quickened.

"You just going to up and leave it all behind?" He drove his point home hard. "Like you left her, Rexanna?"

She jerked back, kicking up her chin. "I don't want to hear any of this from you. Of all people."

His jaw clenched. The words burned through him. She knew what had happened. She didn't have to say so for him to know it. It was there, in the contempt dripping from her words.

"Well, you're hearing it," he gritted. "And if you don't care about your family's legacy, or your place in it, fine. Leave. Go travel the world."

"I'll do that."

"Until you do, you're here, and you'll pitch in with a few chores. Starting with helping out with that herd."

Her back stiffened. "I'm done talking to you." She pivoted, snapped a command to Mack to come with her, then pivoted again to take a few long strides through the grass in the direction of the cabin, leaving him standing there, glowering.

Until she stopped short, lifted one foot, and muttered something unladylike.

"Step in a little scat, Rexanna?" he taunted, moving

toward her.

"So what if I did?" She dragged her foot along the grass to remove the worst of it. "None of your business where I step, anyway."

"Told you to wear shoes."

He bent and scooped her up, one arm behind her knees, the other around her back, catching her unaware. She yelped as he plopped her against his chest and started walking.

Pure stubbornness kept her from hanging on to him, until her sputtering fizzled, she gave up, and flung her arm around his neck.

"If you don't put me down this instant, Roan Bertoletti, I'll—I'll—"

"It's a short walk. You can handle it for that long."

So could he. She didn't weigh much, nothing he couldn't manage, anyway, and he could think of worse things to hold against him.

Still, she was a rigid bundle of arms and legs, and her aggravation took away most of the pleasure he could have had from holding her.

"I'm not one of those helpless actresses who fawn all over you in your movies." She tugged on her dress to keep the hem from flapping up, showing lace.

"Truth in that," he grunted.

"If my grandparents expected me to take care of those alpacas, they would have said so."

"No, they wouldn't. Not yet, anyway."

"Why should you do their talking, then?"

"Because it's only right. They're yours."

"I told you—"

"I know what you said. You're not staying." What a shame, when she could have a fulfilling life on the T

Bar M, something she didn't seem to know or appreciate. "But you're here now. Only right that you pitch in with chores for your own stock."

In all its eccentric-ness, the sorry-looking cabin loomed in front of them, and he halted to set her down. As soon as her shoeless feet touched the ground, she took a fast step back.

"I'll discuss this with my grandparents," she said, her tone frosty.

"You do that. They'll agree with me."

She made an irritated sound. "I have to go."

He nodded. "Supper."

"Bingo."

"Leftovers."

His attempt to bring civility back to their conversation went nowhere. She climbed the steps, Mack on her heels, and went inside. The front door, he thought, shut louder than most folks would find polite.

He sighed, raked a hand through his hair, and encountered the Brylcreem he didn't often use anymore. He scowled. He was getting used to wearing a Stetson without the mess of greasing his hair for show. Made him forget when he did. After rounding his practically new sedan, he climbed behind the wheel and started the engine.

But he didn't put the automobile in gear. A heaviness hung over him, like thick humidity in Kansas heat, oppressive and uncomfortable. He'd come to the ranch to escape, but somehow, by way of her travels, Rexanna knew about the debacle in Hollywood.

She wouldn't know the truth, though.

She wouldn't understand the unfairness.

And now she judged him for both.

His instincts screamed from the certainty. Why else would she have acted with such hostility?

He owed Cord and Harrie an explanation about how he'd made a mess of things after meeting their beloved granddaughter, their only grandchild. They'd agree about the importance of caring for Trixie's stock. They might not agree, though, Roan had taken it upon himself to tell her so.

The whole thing couldn't have gone worse.

Rexanna would have the advantage. At supper, she'd tell them what a jerk he'd been, give them her side of it first, and the stories she'd heard about him, too. Which left Roan trailing behind, eating her dust.

Harrie had invited him over to share those leftovers, and he'd declined. He thought it'd be better for them to have their own time with Rexanna after she'd been gone for so long.

If only he would have accepted.

He had some cleaning up to do, and he couldn't wait to see her again so he could.

Before dawn even cracked across the horizon, Rexanna was done tossing and turning.

The night had dragged along, worsened by her frequent checking of the time. Why had she taken such a long afternoon nap? When before had the hands on her bedside clock crawled as slowly? Would it *ever* be time to get up?

She couldn't escape Roan Bertoletti. He was there in her mind, in the conversation she'd had with her grandparents... in her reluctant regret, too, that she hadn't been nicer to him.

Grandma Harrie had dismissed Rexanna's indignation about the *Film Star Scoop* article. She didn't care one whit about the picture of the injured actress. Hollywood was known for scandalous behavior, she'd declared firmly. They knew how to deceive the American public. The money they made, more than most people could comprehend, thrust those who lived and worked in the movie world into a fantasy life. Glamour and an adoring public filled them with the belief of entitlement that set them apart from the average person and kept them from the reality of what was right and what was wrong.

Despite her outspoken skepticism, she trusted her younger sister, Adelaide, who had done some acting herself, with surprising success, and was a close friend of Roan's father in California. Adelaide had strongly vouched for Roan, and who was Grandma to doubt her own sister? And why should Rexanna doubt her own great-aunt?

Grandma had given her an earful, for sure.

Including how none of that meant Roan had been a part of it. On the day of his arrival at the ranch, he'd been upfront with them. Claimed the stories were false. That he'd been set up. That it was all a sham.

Her grandparents believed every word.

Grandpa wasn't much better. He'd taken Roan's side about the alpacas. She inherited the herd from Aunt Trixie, which made them her responsibility while she was on the ranch. Was it fair for Roan to do the work when she was more than capable? When she was staying right there at her aunt's cabin? He acknowledged her explanation she wouldn't be visiting long, but would she mind helping out in the meantime, if only to keep her mind off of Annie's death and Aunt Trixie's, too?

Rexanna had lost on both fronts.

She knew, too, when to drop the subjects and move on. To respect her grandparents and their beliefs. She'd choked down her roast beef sandwich and Jell-O salad, declined a piece of chocolate cake for dessert, and after helping clear the table and wash dishes, she left.

At least, now they knew about Annie. How her loss had devastated Rexanna, leaving her suffering the biggest failure of her life. Her grandparents had disagreed, saying all the kind and compassionate things she needed to hear and didn't quite believe. Mostly, that Annie had acted on her own, breaking an outfitter's number one rule that no client was to venture into the wilderness alone.

None of that changed the fact that if Rexanna had only taken Annie up the mountain sooner, had been more tolerant of the young woman's need to get her own bear, if she'd just *hurried* more to get her coat and rifle, Annie would still be alive today.

Emitting a little groan, she trampled her guilt down, flung back the pink-and-yellow quilt, and got out of bed. Maybe it was just being here, on her family's ranch, that made the guilt feel more tolerable, but after her restless night, she was compelled by a strong need to redeem herself on more levels than she wanted to admit.

Dressing in a pair of Blue Bell Wranglers and a short-sleeved plaid blouse, she bypassed her hunting boots sitting next to her suitcase and went for her old cowboy boots still in the closet. Wriggling her toes inside the leather, she relived the feel of them on her feet, and how they represented the T Bar M perhaps more than anything else she owned. Memories of mucking stalls, riding her horse, traipsing through mud and manure rushed through her brain, halting time...

Until she shook them off. She'd never live those cowgirl days again, but the boots felt as comfortable as they did when she wore them in her teen years. The soles clomped their familiar clomp across the linoleum floor into the kitchen. She flipped on the light, searched cupboards, and found coffee.

While waiting for two frozen slices of bread to toast, her head tilted to survey the forlorn room, skimming the ceiling, the Kelly-green walls, the drab wallpaper. The white metal cupboards and drawers. The sun-faded curtains and dusty windows.

Aunt Trixie's house needed a thorough cleaning, starting right here in the kitchen.

Mack trotted to the front door. She retrieved a long length of rope from the back end of her Ford and tied him to the porch railing with food and water within easy reach. After finishing her breakfast, she found a bottle of Pine-Sol and a pan under the sink, added plenty of hot water to both, and got to work.

The sun shone high in the sky by the time Rexanna considered the kitchen clean. *Sparkling* clean. A bucket held a mound of rags, proud proof of her efforts. Multiple pans of dirty Pine-Sol water had been tossed outside. Drawers and cupboard shelves were washed, their contents tidied and rearranged. The laundered window curtains hung on the line to dry. No more cobwebs on the ceiling. No more dirt in the corners. No more dust on the window, inside or out.

Aunt Trixie would be pleased.

With her hands on her hips, Rexanna stood in the archway to avoid the wet linoleum floor and surveyed the results. Clean was one thing, but the kitchen needed a fresh coat of paint, too. Maybe a pale yellow, with some pretty new curtains to match. A gingham or flower sprig pattern would give the room a more modern look. She could sew them herself, if Grandma Harrie helped, and before *that* thought went any further, Rexanna banked the whole idea.

There'd be no new curtains or fresh paint while she was here. There simply wouldn't be enough time, and what would be the use?

She wasn't staying.

She swung away with a disconcerted huff. The living room needed her attention next, starting with the rifles and cartridges she'd piled on the couch yesterday. She'd leave the .416 Rigby sheathed. No big game here on the ranch, but her new Weatherby had enough clout in case a wolf or wild boar meandered in to bother the alpacas.

Roan had been by first thing this morning to care for them. Not that he stopped at the cabin to insist she join him, even after his firm declaration of her responsibilities. It had been Mack who alerted her to Roan's arrival, his plum-colored Chrysler an oddity against the rustic barn, and she'd watched him work through the window. The corral was just far enough in the distance to keep her staring, but once the chore was complete, he'd driven off in the other direction.

Her fault. Her not-so-nice attitude kept him away, and she couldn't much blame him, though she found it surprising. He wasn't the kind of man who couldn't hold his own against a woman who was at odds with him, at least, not from what she knew about him.

But then again, what did she really know about him, anyway?

Well, her responsibilities weren't going away, and neither was he. The alpacas would have another feeding this evening, and she'd make sure to be there when they did.

Woo-hooo-wooo! Woo-woo!

Mack's baying howl meant someone had driven out again. Or maybe it was a predator skulking around the corral fence. Now that she knew how one of the alpacas met his demise, and it could easily happen a second time, Rexanna removed the Weatherby from its case and strode onto the porch.

A cowboy in one of the ranch's pickups pulled up in front of the barn with a load of hay and parked. Roan slid out of the truck, giving his Stetson a tug. He unlatched the tailgate, and it would only take one quick glance over his shoulder to find her standing there, staring at him like a schoolgirl. Or an adoring fan. Neither of which she was. Not even close. She escaped back into the cabin with a firm latch of the door behind her.

He might be a pleasure to look at, but he had work to do, and so did she. A gun rack had hung on the wall next to the fireplace for as long as she could remember, displaying her father's favorite Remington hunting weapon. It was the only gun she had of his, and Aunt Trixie promised she would always keep it for her. Rexanna added her Weatherby below it and loved the end result. A cherished set of father-daughter rifles.

Just as she was about to gather the boxes of cartridges off the couch to stack them neatly on a lamp table, the small wooden chest on the mantel sparked her curiosity again. A jewelry box, maybe, though Aunt Trixie wasn't one to wear finery of any kind. Mahogany with brass latches. Antique-looking. Plain, except for an hourglass-shaped mother-of-pearl inlay at its center, and sturdy.

Rexanna had never been allowed to snoop in someone else's belongings, and she wouldn't be snooping now if Aunt Trixie were still alive to explain its presence. Surely, Grandma Harrie would've taken the box home if someone else in the family owned it. All of which left Rexanna to assume the box belonged to her aunt and by way of inheritance was now hers.

She unlatched the case and lifted the lid. Her breath caught. There, nestled amongst a green-velvet lining, glimmered a pink-handled pistol.

Pink.

Definitely made for a woman's hand, and Rexanna couldn't have been more surprised if the little gun rose up off the green velvet and bit her on the nose.

All that prettiness urged her to take the pistol and rest it in her palm, testing its weight. Less than a pound, she guessed. The mother-of-pearl grip shone in pale pink elegance. Surely a custom piece, crafted with pride and skill.

For whom? How long ago? Had some woman consigned a gunsmith to make it for her? Or maybe a husband for his wife? A special gift for a special occasion?

Even more perplexing was why it was here, in Aunt Trixie's cabin. Someone who, as far as Rexanna knew, had never shot a gun in her life because they scared her too much.

Maybe her grandmother knew the history and purpose of the pink pistol. At the very least, Rexanna identified the piece as a .32 caliber Smith & Wesson. A quick spin of the revolver's cylinder showed five chambers, all empty, but a box of smokeless cartridges suggested the pistol would indeed fire at its target.

She twirled the gun around her finger and took imaginary aim out the window with a small smile. No big game shooting with this one. Or even prairie game. Unless someone intended to shoot up close, there wasn't much use for it that she could tell—at least, not for someone like herself. But if nothing else, it was pretty to have and to hold. As gently as if it were a newborn baby, she returned the pistol to its place on the green velvet.

A pocket had been sewn into the lid's lining, and from the slight fullness, something was tucked inside. She could no more stop herself from snooping again than she could fly to the moon, and dipping her fingers into the opening, she withdrew a key on a chain and a folded piece of parchment.

Again, her breath caught, and for a moment, she stared, transfixed by the immensity of what she held. Something old. *Really* old, given the antique shape of the key and its tarnished look. A quick test confirmed the key fit perfectly into the lock. She could only surmise the delicate chain with the key had once been worn by someone, a woman, perhaps. The yellowness of the parchment and the faint mustiness it carried confirmed its age, too, and there was handwriting inside....

Her curiosity raged, and carefully, half-fearing the paper would disintegrate if she handled it with less attention than it deserved, she unfolded the note. Words, written in a man's bold scrawl, but each letter precisely formed for easy reading, captivated her.

She who possesses this pistol possesses an opportunity that must not be squandered. Cast in the tender dreams of maidens from ages past, the steel of this weapon is steadfast and true and will lead an unmarried woman to a man forged from the same virtuous elements. One need only fit her hand to the grip and open her heart to activate the promise for which this pistol was fashioned—the promise of true love. Patience and courage will illuminate her path. Hope and faith will guide her steps until her heart finds its home.

Once the promise is fulfilled, the bearer must release the pistol and pass it to another or risk losing what she has found.

Accept the gift . . . or not.

Believe its promise . . . or not.

But hoard the pistol for personal gain . . . and lose what you hold most dear.

A chill skittered down her spine. The message was just so... profound. Crazy, more. A pistol that would help a woman find love? Was there anything more bizarre than that?

The letter continued. A listing of notes—messages, really—had been written at the end. Different handwriting for each one, and her reading latched onto the first few words:

A gift from the great Annie Oakley...

Rexanna stopped right there.

Her heart lurched in disbelief.

Annie Oakley? The famous sharpshooter whom

she'd admired from the time she first read about her in grade school? Who had been Rexanna's inspiration time and time again to practice, and practice some more, to hit the bullseye as often as she could with her targets?

This pretty pink pistol belonged to *her?*

Rexanna had to start over. Read the parchment again, beginning to end. Surely, she'd misunderstood something along the way. Something this profound, this crazy, she didn't *want* to misunderstand.

The kitchen linoleum was still wet. Reluctant to take time to clear off the couch with all her rifles and ammunition piled on the cushions, the porch was her best option for concentrating, and who wouldn't need some fresh air after this unsettling discovery?

She shut the lid on the mahogany gun case and tucked it under her arm. Carefully re-folding the parchment for easy carrying, she headed out the door.

Roan's pickup was gone, thank goodness. Curled on the grass, Mack opened one eye, then closed it again, lazily returning to his dozing. With barely a glance at Aunt Trixie's hanging things, Rexanna settled on the old wooden bench that had been there for decades and had the weather-beaten look to show for it, she tucked the gun case next to her. After propping her booted feet on the railing, crossing her ankles for extra comfort, she opened the parchment again to re-read the entire message, all the way down to...

A gift from the great Annie Oakley... this pistol carries a legacy of love. If you possess this pistol and find love, please record your name and a bit of your story to encourage those who follow.

Her reading stopped. So that's what the messages

were. Affirmation of the pistol's ability to 'find love.'
Seriously?

The same handwriting continued.

Tessa James married Jackson Spivey on March 3, 1894, in Caldwell, Texas - I was aiming for his heart but accidentally winged him in the arm. Thankfully, forgiveness and love cover a multitude of mishaps.

This woman, Tessa, credited the pistol for falling in love with the man she mentioned, Jackson Spivey, and then married him?

In 1894.

Rexanna didn't know what to think of it.

But drawn like a bird to the trees, she kept reading. The next message held her transfixed, as did the next, and the next....

Collecting trash wasn't the most glamorous job Roan had ever done, but it ranked up there as one of the more important. Like scooping manure out of a stall. Or disposing of an out-of-control wasp nest. Even burying a rotting carcass somewhere out on the ranch. Not doing it wasn't an alternative, and his ego didn't mind, like it might've once, back when he was full of himself, a burgeoning imitation of his father. Getting it done was satisfying and necessary, and it had been one of the first chores Cord had given him when he arrived at the T

Bar M.

Trixie never accumulated much, and on his designated trash day, Roan just added hers to his own before driving around the ranch, collecting more. Afterward, he'd burn everything he had in an old oil barrel up by Cord and Harrie's house, next to the main barn.

The metal can behind Trixie's cabin was only partially filled, likely the cleanup Harrie had done after her passing. Made for easy lifting to drop the contents into the barrel in the back end of the ranch pickup. Freed up the can, too, for more refilling.

He had plans for that trash can. He hoped Rexanna would agree.

He left the truck parked and hefted the can one-handed to the front of the cabin. Seeing Rexanna on the porch, reading a piece of yellowed paper like she'd fallen into a bubble, shutting herself out from the rest of the world, stopped him. He set the trash can on the grass, the action soundless.

Woo-hoo-woo!

Had to be right then, before he had a chance to say anything, that her hound leapt up to greet him.

She jerked, her eyes wide as moons. "You startled me, Roan."

"Not me. Your hound did." He stepped over and gave Mack a rough scratch behind the ears. He could get used to a dog like this one. Friendly and well-behaved.

She lowered her feet and sat straighter on the bench. "Well, you could have said something, you know."

"He beat me to it."

She looked different today. No red-striped housedress or bare feet, but jeans and cowboy boots. She'd pulled her hair back in a braided ponytail, and that right there made her look the most different.

He cocked his hip, taking it all in. She appeared to be right at home, the way she was dressed. A woman who belonged on a ranch.

"Are you here because of the alpacas? It's not time to feed them again, is it?" she asked, calmer.

"No. All done. Until later." Might be she'd spotted him earlier, taking care of them. He'd been sorely tempted to drive over to see her, but then, it was early, and he talked himself right out of it. They hadn't parted on the best of terms last night. He indicated the wooden box next to her. "You found the pink pistol."

She touched the lid, an involuntary acknowledgement. "You know about it?"

"Trixie showed me."

"She did?"

"A while ago."

"Did she show you this?" She held up the yellow paper. "All the women who wrote messages?"

"She told me about them, yeah."

"Marriage Notes."

He shrugged. Wasn't up to him to figure it all out.

"1894, Roan. Clear up to the last one in 1940."

"So I hear."

"Do you realize how long ago that was?"

"A long time." He kept his expression serious. He couldn't decide if she was impressed or ridiculing. Probably both. Acting serious kept him on her side, either way.

Rexanna nibbled on her lower lip. "You don't think

she wrote these messages herself, do you?"

"Made them all up, you mean?"

"Yes. She'd be just crazy enough to do it."

He frowned. "Trixie wasn't crazy."

"Then how do you explain these notes?"

"I can't." And neither could she, that he recalled. "But she believed them."

"I can see why she would." Rexanna's voice lowered, as if she was reluctant to admit the messages were credible at all. "The women who wrote them, well, they seem to be genuinely in love... I assume they're women. The handwriting looks feminine, at least."

"Trixie couldn't fake that."

Her brow lifted. "The handwriting?"

"All different. The paper, too. Where would she get old parchment?"

"I have no idea," Rexanna murmured. "But it's not impossible."

"Suppose not."

Conceding that much, Roan debated changing the subject. Rexanna had a comeback for every argument he made in Trixie's defense. He hadn't moved off the grass, either. Not even an inch, and she didn't know why he'd come yet.

"This whole pink pistol thing is too crazy. I have to think on it." With each movement attentive and careful, she refolded the parchment using the crease lines someone had made before her. "I'll ask my grandmother about it, too. She'll know."

Roan shook his head. "She won't know a thing."

Rexanna paused in her lid-lifting. "Aunt Trixie didn't tell her about the pistol?"

"She did. But Harrie couldn't make sense of it, either. Or Cord. None of us could."

"Oh, for heaven's sake, Roan. Then where did Aunt Trixie get the pistol? Surely, the previous owner knows something."

"We don't know that, either."

She huffed again, her exasperation palpable. "No one knows who the previous owner was? Or where she got the pistol? Is that what you're saying?"

"Nope. And yep." Sympathy cruised through him. She had to be feeling like she was sinking in quicksand. He sure did, at first, until he gave up trying to figure it out. "Trixie claimed it was just there one day. On the mantel. Gun case, key, note, pistol, cartridges. The whole kit and caboodle."

Still holding the folded parchment, she snapped her fingers with her free hand. "Like that."

"So she said."

"No explanation."

"Look, Rexanna. I know how it must sound."

"You have no idea." She slid the parchment into the pocket of the lining, added the key and chain, but didn't close the lid. "Aunt Trixie must have gone to an auction or an estate sale. Maybe she ordered it from a catalog, or something."

He shook his head. He didn't want to refute her argument, but if he didn't, Harrie and Cord would. "She never left the ranch the whole time I was here. She wasn't up to it. As for ordering the gun, your grandparents would know if someone delivered it. And nothing ever came through the mail. They'd know that, too."

"Well, pardon me for saying so, but I don't believe

any of this. It's too ridiculous." Only then did she close the lid.

"The women who wrote those notes would disagree." He regarded her. "How many were there?"

"Seven."

"I'd say seven women who found love and marriage makes pretty good proof the pink pistol works, at least, for them." Roan couldn't exactly say why he was defending the pistol's whimsy. The words just seemed to come right out of his mouth. "Let me see it, will you?"

She opened the lid again, and he moved onto the porch, ducking his head to avoid Trixie's little birdies. Rexanna dipped into the gun case and removed the gun.

"I'll go to the library and research the first woman. Tessa James. Spivey, I mean." She laid the weapon in Roan's outstretched palm. "Maybe there's a news article about her, or something."

Roan declined to discourage her. The Wallace library was too small to be of much help, but if she wanted to try, who was he to stop her? Besides, it'd be interesting to know if she did learn something.

"Pretty thing," he muttered, sliding his thumb over the mother-of-pearl grip, then turning it over to inspect that side, too. As pretty as he remembered. "Doesn't weigh near as much as a Colt."

"Not even close."

He handed it back. "Whatever you think of it, Rexanna, your aunt was taken with the pink pistol. She looked forward to showing it to you some day."

Rexanna's lashes lowered. "Did she say that?"

"Couple of times."

She laid the pistol against the green velvet. The

brass hinges emitted a faint squeak while she closed the lid.

"Now it's yours," he added softly.

"I haven't a clue what to do with it."

"Keep it," he said simply. "That's what she'd want you to do."

"I suppose." She slid her palm over the top of the gun case, like a caress. Thoughtful and slow. "I won't be here long enough to—to dispose of it, so the mantel is the best place for it."

Her admission left a dullness in the pit of his belly. He knew she had a career. Commitments. High-paying clients and a love for the wild. None of that included taking up her old life on the T Bar M.

Two worlds as different as frost and fire.

Neither had anything to do with him, but it was still there, that dullness. He cleared his throat.

"You have lunch yet?" he asked, remembering the trash can he'd brought, still on the grass. Still empty.

"No. Not yet."

"I can make some soup real quick."

"Oh, that's not necessary." She stood.

"I've done it plenty of times." A corner of his mouth lifted. "I know what to do."

He opened the screen door and stepped over the threshold, one booted foot in the cabin, one out on the porch... and halted.

He'd gone into Trixie's cabin so often, he didn't think to ask permission from Rexanna to go in now. Her aunt spent much of her time on the porch, making her little birdies. She'd get so caught up, she'd forget to eat. Whenever Roan wasn't miles out on the ranch, he'd stop by to make sure she would. Wasn't long before it got to be part of his routine.

Now Trixie was gone, and Rexanna changed up his routine, for sure.

"There's a whole bunch of soup in the cupboard," she said, taking the gun case and holding it with both hands, as if she worried she'd drop it, somehow. "You can have your choice."

In a tardy burst of gallantry, he stepped back onto the porch and held the door open wide, giving her plenty of room to pass him and enter the cabin first. She didn't seem to notice how forward he'd been, almost walking in like he owned the place. Might be she didn't feel like the cabin was hers yet, and that was understandable.

He couldn't forget again.

While he latched the screen door, she crossed the living room to set the mahogany box on the mantel, and he kept going into the kitchen, toward the cupboard next to the stove. Didn't take long, and he could see the cleaning she'd done.

"Smells good in here," he said, gaze skimming over the walls he'd swear looked brighter and the window glass that definitely was. Outside, the curtains on the clothesline flapped in the breeze.

From the archway, Rexanna yelped. "Are your boots clean, Roan? You'd better not dirty up this floor."

Again, he didn't move, but his mind raced over the places he'd just been. Grass, mostly. He hadn't left any telltale boot prints behind on the linoleum, and that right there absolved him.

He offered her his most innocent expression. "I didn't. Want me to take my boots off, anyway?"

Apparently satisfied, her inspection lifted from the

flooring, and she continued her walk into the room. "No, but I'll get a rug and put it by the door for next time."

Next time. Liking the sound of that, he relaxed. "Can't tell you how many times my mom asked me that same question."

"Any woman who spent part of her morning scrubbing on her hands and knees is entitled."

She went to the table, covered in oilcloth printed with bold red flowers, and stood there, like she didn't quite know what to do with herself. Might be she wasn't used to having a man with her in someone else's kitchen. Made him wonder if she had someone special in her life. A man she planned to spend the rest of her life with. Someone who loved wild game hunting as much as she did.

Harrie hadn't mentioned anyone, but that didn't mean there wasn't.

More likely, her stiffness came from last night's tiff. Roan had some squaring to do with her, but that could wait. He'd get to it eventually. Her being here, the two of them in the kitchen with lunch in the works, meant she was putting her miff aside, for the time being.

He intended to make the most of it.

Like he'd done numerous times before, he opened the appropriate cupboard door. Rows of red-and-white Campbell's soup cans appeared, each label facing out for easy reading. "What kind do you want?"

"The asparagus, I guess."

"Asparagus, it is." He removed a can of Ox Tail Soup for himself and set both on the table. Removing the opener from a drawer, he unsealed one can, then another. His senses tuned in to her, standing behind him, watching him prepare soup. It wasn't an odd feeling, having people stare at him. Watching. Happened all the time, or, at least, it used to. A film crew, other actors, movie fans. Photographers and beautiful women, even his father, now and again.

Difference was, their staring didn't matter much.

But Rexanna's did.

6

Never once in her life did Rexanna imagine she'd be standing in the same room with a Hollywood actor, let alone someone with the allure of a popular one like Roan Bertoletti. But here she was, and there he was, at the counter working the can opener with a brisk efficiency that made one think he could use it blindfolded.

She attempted to dredge up the disgust she should be feeling for what he'd done to that poor woman. For the affair he'd had with her, too. But the condemnation lay like a limp rag in her stomach and wouldn't come up. Her brain couldn't reconcile what she'd seen in the *Film Star Scoop* magazine with what she was seeing right here in Aunt Trixie's kitchen.

She could barely drag her stare off his broad back or the easy way he moved. Or how thoughtful he was, making her lunch. Had he really come over every day to make sure her aunt ate a decent meal?

Her heart squeezed at his compassion. Her brain warred with the oddity. Right now, Roan was an enigma she couldn't even begin to process, not with him standing only a few yards in front of her, leaving her confused and uncertain.

But riddled with guilt more. While she was away living her dream life, someone else had taken better care of her aunt than she ever had. A stranger, no less. Someone without a shred of Brennan blood in him.

Swallowing hard, choking down the guilt, she moved closer and removed two kettles with their lids from a drawer. Roan dumped her asparagus flavor in one, and she added a can of water. They repeated the process with his beef variety. Roan stirred, and she set the dial on the stove.

"Harrie bought Trixie soup by the case so she wouldn't run out. She ate it every day." He removed two pink Melmac bowls from the cupboard and set them on the table, found spoons, and added them, too.

After Rexanna took the partial loaf of bread from the freezer, the small compartment looked even emptier. If she wanted decent meals while she was here, she'd have to drive into town for a few more groceries, enough to get her by until she had to leave.

She wrinkled her nose. "She didn't get tired of soup all the time?"

"I don't think she noticed."

Rexanna dropped two slices into the toaster and found a jar of Peter Pan peanut butter from the almost-empty cupboard. "That makes me sad."

He shrugged. "She was happy."

Rexanna paused to gather the words before saying them. She exhaled. "Thanks to you."

That she could even make the admission was almost startling. What would Annie think, if she was here? Would her opinion of Roan Bertoletti begin to change, too, if she knew how he cared for Aunt Trixie, and even Rexanna, helping to make lunch? After what he'd done?

What the *Scoop* said he'd done.

"Didn't mind a bit."

"Do you like peanut butter toast? I should have asked."

"Grew up on it. Make four, will you? I'm hungry."

His smile could've melted the peanut butter in the jar, it was that charming, and Rexanna turned away. She didn't want to be affected by him or his smile or how he seemed to overpower the little kitchen with the sheer magnitude of his presence.

She forced herself to concentrate on slathering the warm toast with the peanut butter, turning it almost gooey, every time the bread popped up. By the time she'd stacked a pink plate, their soup had heated through.

"Mind if we put both pots on the table and serve them from there?" Roan asked. "Saves washing extra dishes."

Again, she had to steel herself against the power of his grin. It could've glowed, that grin, like moonlight over snow, and she dredged up her best attempt to fight it. She set the plate of toast on top of the oilcloth, still bright with its red flowers, even after years of after-meals wiping.

"You're probably used to starched tablecloths, with fine china and candles, and with—with caviar, or something," she said, straight-shouldered.

His brow shot up. "For lunch?"

"Or dinner. Even breakfast, too." She hung on tight to her sarcasm, but her accusations sounded unfair, even to her. "Not soup and toast in an old, worn-out kitchen."

He dropped a hot pad onto the oilcloth and set the kettle holding her asparagus soup on top. He pulled out the chair in front of her.

"Sit," he said.

He hadn't used that tone of voice with her before. Brisk and firm. Giving her clear warning he wouldn't tolerate her refusal.

Was that how he'd spoken to the young woman before they'd quarreled, before her tumble down the stairs? Maybe, or maybe not, but Rexanna felt no fear with him. No sensing of malice, either, from the coolness in his voice.

"Fine," she said, in the same brisk tone.

She moved to comply. What would she gain from refusing when lunch was hot and ready, besides appearing ungrateful and haughty, of which she felt neither?

He moved the chair beneath her as she sat, the gesture so *gentlemanly* her eyes stung unexpectedly. The memory of her father doing the same for her mother reared into her mind, and Grandpa for Grandma, too. Two men who were honest and upright and loved their wives beyond measure.

Not even Damien afforded her such gallantry, and he knew her better than anyone.

Roan returned with a second hot pad and the ox tail soup. After hooking his Stetson on the back of the chair, he ladled soup into both of their bowls, then sat, too.

"My mother met my father when she was on a family vacation to New York City. Went to the premiere of one of his movies, *Hold Your Man* with Clark Gable and Jean Harlow. Dad was just making a name for himself, then," he said quietly. "Mom was one of Clark Gable's biggest fans. She wanted to meet him. Met my father instead. They spent a little time together, and when she headed home to the family ranch, she was pregnant with me."

"Oh." Rexanna's gaze lowered to her soup. "How did that go over with her family?"

"Not good."

"I wouldn't think so."

"My grandfather was furious. Insisted my father marry Mom and give her respectability or he'd sue. Scandal at that point in my father's career was the last thing he wanted. Or needed."

Rexanna chewed on a bite of toast. "So, did he? Marry her?"

"Yes. Took her out to Los Angeles. They both tried to make the marriage work, she told me once. But she didn't fit into his world. They were like apples and..." He paused, as if searching for the right comparison. "...lobster." Matter-of-fact, Roan swallowed a spoonful of soup.

"That's different, all right." She hid a smile.

"She couldn't abide the immorality that many of his friends took for granted. She felt inferior to the beautiful women who never failed to catch his eye. His cheating humiliated her. They divorced by the time I was two."

"That's too bad," Rexanna said and meant it.

"I grew up on her family's ranch. She never got over her failed marriage. Never felt like she was good enough for a man. Eventually, my grandparents passed away, and her depression got worse. I was fourteen when she died."

A little sound of commiseration slid from her throat. "I was fifteen when my parents died."

Would he know that already? Had Grandma Harrie told him as much?

The admission came out without her conscious thought. The realization they had the loss of their parents at a similar age in common, well, her heart softened over it.

"Tough time for a kid. That age and all," he said.

"Very." Somber, she nodded.

"My father took me to California with him. I hated Los Angeles, at first. Missed the kids at my old school. I'd wanted to graduate with them. Take over my grandparents' ranch. It was the future I always thought I'd have."

"But you learned to love Los Angeles?"

"Not love it, but I accepted it." He shrugged. "I was Roan, Sergio Bertoletti's son. The film world respected me for that. I looked like him. Acting came natural to me. Most times, it felt silly saying things I'd never say, or doing things I'd never do, but I could follow a script and earned a decent living. I wanted to buy my own ranch someday with the money."

Rexanna held her breath. Now came the part where he'd tell her about the injured woman, wouldn't it? The reason why he left Los Angeles?

"Hope I'm not boring you with all this, Rexanna—"

"You're not," she said quickly.

"—but you need to know the person I am. I'm more cowboy than actor. I'm more my mother's son than my father's. I appreciate a fancy restaurant with all the trimmings as much as anyone. But I'd rather eat soup and peanut butter toast with you."

She blinked at the admission. His low voice rumbled with earnestness, an intimacy that slid through her veins and warmed her blood. She tried to hang onto her resentment but failed.

He made it too easy to believe him.

Was that his acting skill, too? Did he hope she'd be like any gullible female, infatuated with his Mediterranean good looks and movie star reputation?

Or as gullible as her family? Her grandparents, especially?

If he did, he was sorely wrong.

If he didn't, the fault was all hers, and he left her floundering in confusion like a carp on the beach.

"Point taken," she said quietly.

"Good. Subject closed."

He'd eaten the entire pot of ox tail soup himself. Only one more piece of toast remained, and he was already reaching for it....

"Can I get you anything else?" she asked. "There's some of my asparagus soup left."

"Nah." He paused before taking a bite. "Unless there's some of Trixie's gumdrop cookies around."

She frowned. "I didn't see any."

"Too bad." A big bite of toast disappeared into his mouth, puffing his lean cheek. "She didn't make them very often. Surprised me when she did." His sooty eyes glimmered with humor. "She let me eat as many as I wanted. Tended to spoil me that way."

"Gumdrop cookies." She cocked her head, studying him.

"What?" He drew back with an innocent expression. "You don't think they're my style, either?"

Her mouth opened to defend herself by declaring that anyone could like gumdrops, even Hollywood actors playing cowboys, but Mack's baying howl jerked her attention to the window, instead.

"Must be someone here," Roan said, looking out, too.

"Probably just a squirrel Mack wants to chase."

But through the freshly washed panes, a tan, red-topped station wagon shone through a cloud of dust, passing by too quickly for either of them to make an identification.

"In a hurry, whoever he is," Roan muttered and headed toward the front door.

Rexanna scrambled out of her chair to follow. "You don't recognize the car?"

"No one on the ranch has a red top that I've seen." He stepped onto the porch and made a long-legged descent to the ground to get a better look at that cloud, fast dissipating down the road.

"Someone visiting my grandparents, maybe." Rexanna halted on the top step behind him.

"The main house is that way." He jerked a thumb in the opposite direction. "Someone's trespassing."

Rexanna pursed her lips. Anyone on T Bar M land without permission broke her grandfather's number one rule. It'd been that way since the day she was born and long before then, too. No rancher wanted intruders on their property, not with livestock to protect, and a whole slew of other reasons, besides.

"I'll mention it to Cord," Roan said. He rubbed his jaw, as if the whole thing troubled him.

But the gesture struck a quick surge of sympathy through Rexanna. As a wild game hunter, she knew full well the importance of acquiring permission from a landowner. That this person hadn't, well, it wasn't the end of the world.

Still, it went deeper for Roan, and Rexanna couldn't put her finger on a reason why. Her scrutiny lingered over him, noting how thick his hair was, of all things. Without the Brylcreem, its thickness was far more appealing as it gleamed in the sun. A lock had fallen casually over his forehead, giving him a look not so different from Elvis Presley.

And her belly curled.

He turned toward her, and she yanked back her staring, blinking fast to hide that she was.

"You get enough for lunch?" he asked, his voice low. Appealing.

Relieved that he'd put his concerns for the trespasser aside, she nodded. "Plenty, yep."

"There's some yardwork that needs to be done." He indicated the empty trash can he'd brought, still sitting on the grass. "Thought we'd get right to it."

"We?" She didn't move. "That's why you came out

here? To make me work with you?"

"Plenty to do around here. Figured cleaning up all the dead leaves and old grass would be a good start on this yard."

She didn't need to pull her gaze off him to know he spoke the truth. The chore had been on her list, but Roan just moved it clear to the top. Her original plan to clean the living room would have to wait.

"I'll help," he added.

"You don't have to," she said quickly, guessing he took her slow response for reluctance. "I know how to pull weeds."

"So do I." His mouth curved. "It'll go faster with the two of us. You want to wash dishes first, or do you want me to?"

No chore seemed beneath him, and she hadn't expected it. Rexanna could barely recall her own father washing dishes. Or Grandpa, either. Not often, anyway.

"I'll do it," she said softly. "It won't take long."

"Helps to serve soup right out of the kettle, remember?" He smiled, and her belly did that funny curl all over again.

Her own smile came all by itself. "I do."

"I'll get started on the yard, then." He bent to rub Mack's head affectionately. "You'll keep me company, won't you, buddy?"

Well aware her hound seemed to forget her when Roan was around to shower him with attention, Rexanna went back into the cabin. The mahogany gun case with its pink pistol inside held reign on the mantel, but she kept walking, straight into the kitchen.

Roan pulled up behind his plum-colored Chrysler, parked, and cut the pickup's engine. After sliding out from behind the wheel, he locked the door and pocketed his keys. As far as he knew, no one else on the ranch secured their vehicles, but locking up was a habit he'd brought from Los Angeles. It'd been a big change to switch from a crowded city with homes and apartments crammed onto every block to living out here on the ranch's wide-open spaces by himself. But it was a change he welcomed. Craved more. In his prouder moments, he could even convince himself he belonged out here.

The T Bar M Ranch.

Rexanna's family's home for generations, just like the one he'd grown up on.

No wonder he felt like it was a part of him.

He strode past his sedan and climbed the pair of steps to the small porch leading to the front door of his cabin. But he didn't go inside. The old line camp shack had once given T Bar M cowboys a place to stay when they were out riding fence or tending cattle. Now, Roan called the place home.

The shack hadn't been much to look at when he arrived from California. It sat empty for years, and Kansas weather and critters had taken their toll. Those days, he would've slept on dirt to get away from the trouble he was in. The anger that kept burning through him, too. But Cord and Charlie had been unaffected and quick to help him fix up the place. The scent from fresh-cut lumber still lingered in the two rooms that made up the cabin. A faint paint smell with it. It was all he needed, those two rooms. They'd become his haven.

He leaned a shoulder on the porch's post and

narrowed an eye over the rangeland sprawling in front of him. The red-topped station wagon clouded in dust wouldn't leave his memory. His gut insisted that whoever was driving was a stranger to these parts. The locals knew not to trespass, that there was no acceptance of it. Everyone around knew where Cord and Harrie lived, too. Why else would anyone come onto the ranch except to see them?

Only a stranger who drove in for his own purposes and with no understanding of a rancher's intolerance. A purpose that didn't involve Cord and Harrie.

Who, then? And why?

Roan didn't want to think the stranger was looking for him. That the debacle Roan had left behind in Los Angeles somehow resurrected itself and came back to haunt him in Wallace, Kansas.

Made him a little sick from the possibility, for sure.

Best Roan could hope for was the stranger had gotten himself good and lost with no intention of driving onto the T Bar M. That once he realized his mistake, he found his way back onto the highway again and left for good.

Mostly, Roan hoped his worrying was a waste of time.

He straightened, lifted his hat and raked a weary hand through his hair, then re-settled the Stetson on his head. He'd much rather think about Rexanna and being with her this afternoon, pulling weeds and raking old leaves, of all things. She was a hard worker, a trait she clearly inherited from the Brennan family, and it'd been a real pleasure getting the job done together. By the time they finished, the trash can was full, and the old foundation around Trixie's cabin hadn't looked as good since he'd arrived.

Afterward, he showed her a few specifics about feeding the alpacas. Hay and minerals and what part of the corral she'd need to clean up after them. She took to that, too, and wasn't long, he didn't have much reason to stick around. Not that she asked him to, and with supper calling for both of them, she went her way, and he went his.

He sighed and straightened from the porch post. An unusual restlessness settled over him, and he figured Rexanna had a big part in him feeling that way. Her place was easy enough to see from his porch. Too far away to be neighborly, but close enough to keep him thinking about her. Knowing she was there, and he was here, well, it didn't help his restlessness a bit.

He had the whole night ahead of him. Alone. Never used to bother him, being alone, but tonight would be different.

7

The Next Morning

"Get in, Mack."

Rexanna held the Ford's door open, and her coonhound hopped onto the seat with his usual speed and grace. Before shutting the door, she cranked the window partway down. What dog didn't love to hang his head out while driving down the road?

After closing the passenger side door, she climbed into the driver's seat, set her purse and grocery list aside, and started the engine. The morning sun had already warmed the steering wheel, and she rolled her window down, too, freeing the stuffiness captured within the cab.

The truck moseyed out of the drive toward the road leading to her grandparents' house, but Rexanna didn't accelerate, lingering instead to study the road in the opposite direction.

The direction Roan had taken home last night.

She knew of the old line camp. Hearing that he'd fixed it up into livable quarters turned her soft and appreciative inside. The shack was a part of her family's history dating back to her great-grandparents, Trace and Morgana McCord, the original owners of the T Bar M. After Harrie and Cord took over, the spread had flourished into the sprawling and successful cattle operation it was today.

Where was Roan now?

He hadn't been over to feed the alpacas this morning, but then, they were in her care now. At least, for as long as she'd be staying on the ranch. Why would he come over, anyway? There were plenty of other chores waiting for him, none of which had anything to do with her.

It was silly to be thinking about him, anyway.

She wasn't staying.

He was.

What was the point in wondering where he was or what he was doing?

She blew out a breath, tucked her hair behind her ear, and turned the pickup the other way, arriving at her grandparents' two-story house to find Grandma in the back, hanging towels on the clothesline. Her housedress and apron fluttered in the breeze while she worked, her

back to the road, and her wicker basket in front of her.
Rexanna put the pickup in Park and propped her elbow on the open window. "Hey, Grandma!"
Her grandmother turned in surprise. "Where are you going, Rexi?"
"To Perelman's Grocery. Do you need anything?"
She strode a few steps closer. "No, I have plenty. Why don't you come in? Take what you need from the pantry."
"I want to go to the library, too."
"Do you have enough money for groceries?"
Rexanna laughed. It was just like her to worry about such a thing, as if Rexanna was twelve again. "You don't need to give me any money for groceries, Grandma, but can I borrow your library card?"
"Of course." She appeared so taken aback that Rexanna held her breath in case she asked why she needed it. "Tell Cecelia I said you could. She has my information in her files."
"Thanks. I won't be gone too long." She put the truck in Drive again.
But her grandmother strode even closer. "Roan said he went over to your cabin yesterday."
Just hearing his name dropped a flutter into her belly. "He did."
"And you had lunch together." Her nut-brown eyes sparkled.
"We did." Rexanna didn't know if she should be amused or exasperated that she'd been their topic of discussion. "I suppose you know what we ate, too?"
"Soup and peanut butter toast." Her smug expression elicited Rexanna's laugh. "And you pulled weeds together."

Together. The lone word spoke volumes, and Rexanna sobered.

"Filled the whole trash can, yep." She hesitated. Whatever Grandma was thinking, or leading up to, or was hopeful of, Rexanna had to put an end to it. "There was work to be done, that's all. Anyone would have done it, and—"

"He's a nice boy, Rexanna."

Her grandmother's quiet voice held a thread of earnestness, as if it were imperative that Rexanna believe her, and Rexanna almost choked.

Boy?

Roan Bertoletti was all man, without a shred of boy left in him, and if Grandma had an ulterior motive in pointing his *niceness* out, well, Rexanna wasn't ready to be quite as gullible as her just yet.

Her trip to the library would clear up any gullibleness, unfortunately.

"I'd better get going, Grandma. See you later, okay?" The pickup's tires rolled forward.

"Drive carefully, honey. Oh, and Rexi?"

Rexanna braked again, twisting to see her grandmother through the window.

"Would you like to go riding this afternoon? Maybe Roan could go with you."

Her belly curled again from that betraying flutter. Why did the man's name affect her like that? "I'd love to ride, but not with Roan. Grandpa hired him for ranch chores, not to entertain me."

It might be the words came out a bit sharper than she intended, but she didn't stick around to hear her grandmother's response. The pickup accelerated a little faster than was polite, and after driving through the T

Bar M crossbar onto the highway, spraying gravel, Rexanna succumbed to an exasperated scowl.

What had gotten into Grandma, anyway? Trying to play matchmaker with Roan and her? It wasn't like they were a good fit for one another. Two people couldn't be more different, and a Hollywood actor was the farthest thing from Rexanna's idea of the perfect man in her life, besides.

Even if he was a T Bar M cowboy more.

Regardless, it was a side of her grandmother she'd never seen before, let alone comprehended, and if Rexanna didn't know better, she might even believe that silly pink pistol on the mantel had something to do with it.

Rexanna maneuvered the Ford into the angled parking place in front of the Wallace Public Library and cut the engine. She hadn't been inside the small brick building since she was a kid, and memories washed over her as vividly as if she were already inside. The creaky old floor and tall windows and all those shelves of books which had so often fueled her dreams of traveling the world. Within the plastered walls, she'd learned of wild game animals and firing arms. Exotic countries and native peoples. Where would the world be without libraries and the wealth of knowledge they contained?

All kinds of information for all kinds of readers, and there was nowhere else in Wallace that would have what she needed.

"Stay here, Mack," she said, giving the coonhound an affectionate head rub. Not that he seemed to notice, given all the new things he could look at through his open window. "I'll be right back."

She gathered up her purse, leaving her grocery list on the seat, and exited the cab. Though the library was located a couple of blocks off Main Street, every parking spot was taken. Mama Jane's Diner was a popular draw, given that it would be lunch time soon. So was the hardware store and Perelman's Grocery, a little farther down. Townspeople strolled up and down the sidewalks, holding her dog's attention. She climbed the cement stairs and went inside.

As far as she could tell, nothing had changed in the time she'd been gone. The thin brown carpet, the long tables and chairs, even the librarian's desk on the right side of the main room were just as she remembered. Cecilia Hansen was still there as head librarian, too, as much of a fixture as the books themselves. No one knew the Wallace Public Library better than she did.

The librarian glanced up from her book sorting. "Rexanna Brennan? Is that you?"

Like it'd been for the past two decades, her hair was tightly permed but grayer since the time Rexanna had seen her last. She was more matronly, too. But her expression was friendly, and her red lipstick still perfectly applied.

"How are you, Mrs. Hansen?" Rexanna kept her voice hushed, a rule the librarians strictly enforced.

"I'm just fine. I'm sorry to hear about your Aunt Trixie, bless her heart."

"Thank you."

"She was the sweetest soul. I hadn't seen much of her before she passed, though. You came back for her funeral, didn't you?"

"I did, yes." Not only was Mrs. Hansen efficient in managing books, she was efficient in keeping track of everyone's lives, too. Rexanna had to hurry to change the subject, or she'd have to give the woman a rundown of her own life. "I'd like to do some research on a couple of things. Are the title cards and magazines still in the back by the window?"

"They are. We haven't moved them in years. Unfortunately, our cataloging isn't as useful as it could be. The foundation funding is getting so difficult to obtain, and we are too small to justify much spending." Not surprisingly, she rose. "Which magazine are you looking for? We don't carry as many as we used to, you know."

"Oh, don't bother to get up," Rexanna said, avoiding her question. Which made no sense, because the woman would find out anyway when it came time to check out. "I can find them."

"I hope we have the issue you're looking for. We pull them if they get too out-of-date."

As if Rexanna hadn't spoken, she left her desk and headed briskly toward the windows, leaving Rexanna with little choice but to follow. The thin carpet muffled their footsteps until they reached the magazines hanging by dowels on a wooden rack.

"Which magazine, Rexanna?" Mrs. Hansen waited expectantly.

The red logo leapt upward from the rest and seared Rexanna's memory, throwing her back to that horrible afternoon at Kodiak Island while she was on the St. Brendan yacht with Annie.

"*Film Star Scoop,*" she said, feeling almost guilty for saying it.

"The *Scoop*." She plucked one in particular off the rack. "The issue about Roan Bertoletti?"

Rexanna blinked her surprise. "How did you guess?"

"Oh, everyone in town has read this issue. It's practically falling apart. We would have thrown it out long ago if folks weren't so interested."

"I see."

She frowned.

So did Mrs. Hansen.

"Some of the stories in these magazines are rigged, Rexanna, if you don't mind me saying so. They'll say anything to make money."

"Rigged?" Rexanna drew back.

"It's what those high-falutin' movie studios out in California do to the actors and actresses working for them. They make up stories to protect them or destroy them." She sniffed. "Depending on the circumstances, of course."

"That can't be true."

In all the years Rexanna had known Mrs. Hansen, not once had she ever doubted anything the woman had said. She was, after all, one of the smartest people in Wallace.

But everyone had to be wrong sometime, and Rexanna was certain now was one of those times for Mrs. Hansen.

Before she could remind the librarian of the picture Annie had showed her of the poor actress's injuries, or that the actress herself claimed Roan had pushed her down the stairs, Mrs. Hansen pointed a chubby finger at her.

"In Roan's case, they wanted to destroy him." She

clucked her tongue in disgust. "It wasn't fair to him, but all of us here in Wallace can see through their shameless scheme. The whole story is a lie."

The printed story warred with Rexanna's need to discern the truth. "How do you *know* that?"

"Because we know Roan. He's as fine as they come. Your grandfather wouldn't have taken him in if he wasn't."

If Rexanna didn't know any better, she'd swear Mrs. Hansen was in cahoots with Grandma, singing the man's praises, putting him on the proverbial pedestal, falling for his dark Mediterranean looks and charm... and yet, when before had Rexanna doubted her grandparents in anything they'd done? The decisions they'd made?

In the time she'd known him, what had Roan done to convince her he was anything less than honorable? Capable of doing what the actress claimed he'd done?

"Besides, what man would push one woman down the stairs and then give another the care and compassion that Roan gave to your Aunt Trixie?" Mrs. Hansen demanded.

Rexanna didn't move, didn't breathe. The words circled in her brain and held her feet riveted on the brown carpet. Not a single word formed to defend herself. Not a lone piece of logic reared up to counter Mrs. Hansen's.

"Read the article and decide for yourself if it's true." As if she understood Rexanna's confusion, her expression turned kindly and her voice softer. "I think you'll agree with the rest of us." She straightened with her librarian smile. "Now, then. Take all the time you need with the title cards. I hope you find our cataloging helpful. I'm here to assist if you need me."

"Thank you."

"Your library card would have expired by now. Would you like to use your grandmother's card, instead, to borrow the magazine?"

Feeling like a recalcitrant child, Rexanna gathered her dignity and lifted her chin. "Yes, please."

But Mrs. Hansen was already headed toward her desk, efficient in knowing exactly what Rexanna needed.

Well, Roan was right. Rexanna had no luck in her research on the woman named Tessa James Spivey, who wrote the first Marriage Note and claimed the first benefits of the pink pistol's matchmaking prowess. Even after enlisting Mrs. Hansen's help—without giving any details, of course—Rexanna's search turned up empty. Despite her obvious friendship with Annie Oakley, it was like Mrs. Spivey didn't exist.

Except she did. Rexanna had seen her handwriting herself. Her Marriage Note had been clear, intriguing, and quite romantic.

Defeated by the dead end, Rexanna waved goodbye to Mrs. Hansen and left. Her descent down the library stairs faltered at the sight of the man standing next to her Ford pickup, lavishing Mack with plenty of head rubs and neck scratches.

Mack's tongue lolled out the side of his mouth, as if he'd been elevated into heaven. But seeing her, he howled his baying *woo-woo,* and the startled stranger whirled toward her. Rexanna clutched the rolled-up issue of *Film Star Scoop* in her fist and met him on the sidewalk. She didn't have time to fathom why she didn't want him to see what she'd checked out of the library. An instinctive thing, hiding it, like her guilt. As if she was betraying Roan by reading about him and the drama surrounding his scandalous fall from Hollywood society.

"Well, hello-o," the stranger said, turning toward her with an arrogant grin and an even more outrageous sweep of her body, from her boots up to the barrette in her hair.

She refused to be affected by him. A ladies' man, no doubt. A player any woman would be a fool to trust.

"Can I help you with something?" she asked coolly.

He tipped up his fedora, gray like his suit. "This your truck?"

"It is." She didn't appreciate how he leaned against the hood, like he had ownership of it. "My dog, too."

"He's a beauty." Again, he leveled her with a dallying gaze. "Like you."

"I repeat, can I help you with anything?"

"Nope. But I'd like to take your picture."

"My picture."

"With you and your dog."

She cocked her head and leveled him with her most cynical stare. "Why would I do that?"

He reached inside his suit coat and pulled out a pack of Camels, shook one out, and tucked it, unlit, in the corner of his mouth. His tie hung loosely from his white shirt collar, exposing a thin throat. Scrawny, almost. "Because that's what I do. Take pictures. And you're a beautiful woman."

She'd bet her prized Rigby rifle he didn't live in

Wallace. He carried a big city air about him that didn't fit in her small town, populated with mostly farmers and ranchers who wouldn't be so brazen with one of their own. Especially a woman.

"I don't think so." She stepped around him and headed toward the driver's side of her truck. Perelman's was less than a block away, but she refused to leave Mack alone around this guy. She'd drive to the grocery store, if she had to. "You're not from around here, are you?"

He swiveled to face her over the hood. "Just passing through."

"Taking pictures."

"Don't believe me?" He spoke around the cigarette, as if he'd forgotten it was still there.

"Why should I?" He was just arrogant enough to feed her a line, expecting her to fall at his feet in a swoon.

"I'll show you." He took a pair of steps toward the station wagon parked next to her. A tan Chevrolet with a red top. He opened the passenger door, leaned in, and pulled out a camera, complete with flash. He faced her again, grinning around that cigarette. "See? Proof."

But that red top held Rexanna's interest more.

Took some effort to hold in her suspicions and focus on him.

"Are you wanting to take pictures of other things around here, besides me?" she demanded.

"Whatever I can get." He shrugged. "I'm working on a story."

"What kind of story?"

"You know, about people. I'd love to have you in it, honey."

"I'll bet you would. And I'm not your *honey*." She yanked open the driver's door and got in, setting her purse and the rolled-up magazine close beside her. "Your story's not going to happen."

He squatted to see her through the open window, leaning a bit sideways to avoid Mack, taking up most of the view.

"How about lunch, then? Mama Jane's, right across the street. Sign in the window says a free slice of pie today. Noon special."

"Nope."

"Aw, c'mon. Won't take long. Your dog will be fine."

It wasn't Mack she was worried about. "What's your name, anyway?"

He pulled out the cigarette. Finally.

"Kelly," he said. "What's yours?"

"Ever hear of a place called the T Bar M?" she asked.

He drew back, so slightly she might not have noticed. Like a tiger in the wild, tensing before he pounced.

"Might've. Big ranch around here, right?" he said with a brittle casualness.

"No reason for you to be on it."

His expression shuttered. "Who said I was?"

"Ranchers don't appreciate trespassers. They'll shoot. Trust me."

His Adam's apple bobbed in his scrawny neck. "That right?"

"Consider yourself warned." She started the engine, pushed in the clutch, reversed, and pulled out of the angled parking space. In the moments it took to brake, then shift into Drive, she helped herself to a healthy glimpse of the red-topped station wagon's license plate, yellow letters and numbers on black background, and her worst suspicions roiled in her stomach.

Kelly, the photographer, was here, all the way from California.

And Rexanna had a sickening feeling she knew why.

8

Later That Afternoon

Roan reined in at the front of Rexanna's cabin. It'd become too easy thinking of the place as hers now. Legally, it was, but in his mind, she chased away the clouds Trixie had lived under for so long and brightened the house with new life. Like sunshine sprayed over the roof and lawn, warming the air with a sweet welcome.

He dismounted and tied the reins to his buckskin to the porch's post, then stepped around to do the same with the cream-colored mare he'd brought. Rexanna might be interested in knowing the young horse was foaled from one she used to ride as a kid. Seemed only right that she ride her this afternoon, if she was so inclined. For old times' sake.

He approached the stairs, and after taking the first one, he paused in approval from the color around the foundation. She'd planted flowers this afternoon, giving more new life. Made him glad they cleaned out all the dead weeds and overgrown grass yesterday. A huge difference, for sure, those little bursts of color.

A woman's touch. Just what the cabin needed.

After climbing the stairs, he dipped his head to keep his Stetson from hitting Trixie's little birdies and knocked on the door. Through the screen, the aroma from whatever she had in the oven reached him, and that was a nice change, too. Toward the end, Trixie had pretty much quit using the oven at all.

Rexanna stood at the kitchen counter, engrossed in whatever she was making. He liked how she wore her Wranglers snug around her hips and thighs, shaping her slim, athletic build. A sleeveless blouse in bright green and maroon plaid was tucked in at her waist, and he couldn't keep standing here, on the outside looking in, like some kind of peeping tom, enjoying the womanly picture she made. At his knock, her head swiveled toward him, and for a moment, their gazes held.

She hadn't been expecting him, and maybe the reason she didn't move indicated her surprise. But there was some power in her gaze, and it kept him from moving, too.

"Come on in, Roan," she said finally, dissipating the power she held over him. "The door's not locked."

He pulled on the latch and went in. Mack lay in

front of the living room window and barely stirred from his dozing. Only the opening of one eye indicated he knew Roan had arrived, but he was too lazy to give him a howl of welcome like he usually did. Roan kept walking, through the living room and into the kitchen, his boot soles a steady clomp across the linoleum.

"Smells good in here," he said, his voice low with appreciation. "What're you making?"

"Roasted chicken in the oven. Jell-O salad here." She swirled the orange gelatin with her index finger, going back and forth over the bottom of the glass dish. "Just getting it dissolved." Lifting her finger, she shook off the dripping Jell-O and took the dish in both hands, avoiding the use of her orange-tipped finger. "Open the refrigerator door, will you?"

He complied and stepped aside, giving her room. An assortment of groceries filled the shelves. Milk, eggs, butter, a half-bag of apples, and a few vegetables. A six-pack of bottled beer, too. Even the refrigerator benefited from her presence. Sparkling clean and welcoming.

Bending, she slid the glass dish toward the middle of the metal rack, careful to avoid sloshing the gelatin. Afterward, she scooped up a bag of carrots and a bundle of celery held together with a rubber band and shut the door with her hip.

"Thirty minutes. I can't forget," she said, mostly to herself.

"Better set the timer."

"I better, yes."

She stepped to the stove, but he moved in front of her before she could get there.

"How're you going to set the dial with your hands

full?" he murmured, his tone teasing. "Jell-O on your finger, to boot."

She stood there, slender and womanly, with her cheeks pinkened from the warmth in the kitchen. Her barrette had slipped, too, allowing her blonde hair to fall over one side of her forehead.

Made him want to slide his whole hand into that mane of hair and brush it all back. To learn the feel of its weight. The satiny feel, too.

Instead, he took her wrist, compelling her to shuffle the vegetables against her chest with her free arm, and lifted her orange-tipped finger into his mouth. His tongue stroked her skin, over and around, until the orangey-tart taste was gone.

She drew in a shaky breath and breathed his name, a pathetic attempt at protest. Not that it did any good. He didn't pull away, and she didn't, either, and he'd swear she trembled, as if he affected her in a way she hadn't expected.

It pleased him, how he affected her, and he didn't want to figure it all out yet.

But he might've overstepped his bounds, and in no hurry, he released her.

"I'll take these while you wash up," he said, holding the carrots and celery with one hand. With the other, he set the timer on the stove. "You need help cutting anything up?"

"No, thanks." She dried her hands on a towel and regarded him. "How come you're not working?"

"Your grandfather gave me the rest of the afternoon off."

"He did, did he?"

She sounded skeptical, and his brow arched. "Hey,

we go to work early. Already put in a full day's work."

"But plenty of time left to ride horses."

Her cool tone warned her mood was off. So much for surprising her with the cream-colored mare.

"You don't want to go riding with me?" he asked, moving aside so she could open a drawer and pull out a grater.

"Not if Grandma is making you take me."

"She's not." His brain scrambled to turn the truth into an explanation she'd accept. "Well, she suggested it, and I was happy to oblige. Why would I refuse? I didn't have anything else to do, and it's a nice day."

"So now I'm just a way to help you pass the time."

He frowned. Warning bells went off in his head for the snit she was in. If he had any sense, he'd keep his mouth shut from here on out.

"I don't want you to babysit me while I'm here," she said, heading to the sink.

"Babysit you?"

He hooked a thumb in the hip pocket of his Levi's while the words rolled through him. She wasn't like this last night while they worked in the yard. What made her different now?

"Look, Roan, I'm too busy." She rinsed a stalk of celery and several carrots under running water. "The chicken won't be done for a while yet, and I have to keep an eye on the Jell-O, or it will set too much. I have to add the vegetables at just the right time or—"

"I'll wait."

He wasn't having any more of her excuses. He needed to figure her out and give her some space. If he'd done something to make her mad, she needed to 'fess up so he could make things right with her.

"I'll take Mack outside and throw a ball to him," he said.

He had no idea if Rexanna had dog toys or not, but he'd find a stick, if he had to. Afterward, he'd invite himself to stay for dinner. If she didn't toss him out on his nose, they could talk it out, at least.

With nothing but the sound of running water for her answer, he helped himself to an apple from a fruit bowl on the table, and it was only then he saw what she'd been reading.

The magazine lay on the oilcloth, its pages open to the article that had almost destroyed him. The picture of Doreen Adams and her swollen face sickened him still, and in a burst of anger, of barely-suppressed frustration, he snatched the magazine and slapped it closed. If he hadn't clung to self-control, he would've thrown the thing across the room.

Now, everything made sense.

Now, he understood.

Of everyone, he thought Rexanna, the granddaughter of Cord and Harrie, two of the finest people he'd ever known, who had treated him with fairness and compassion and a complete lack of judgement, would have done the same.

He thought wrong.

He whirled toward her, still standing at the sink and watching him. Some of the color had left her cheeks. After shutting off the faucet, she dropped the celery and the carrots in the sink, and slowly turned toward him, her hands dripping.

"Roan," she said quietly. "Look, I—"

"Are you going to be like the rest of them, Rexanna?" he growled. "Gossipmongers who eat up this—" he refrained from using a crass word better suited to his thinking "—*stuff* and believe everything they read?"

"I didn't know what to think. That's why I—"

"Lies. Every word." Disgusted, he dropped the apple back into the bowl.

"I needed to read the article. It seemed to be the place to start. Ever since Annie showed it to me...." Her voice trailed off.

Annie. The young woman who'd been killed by the bear in Alaska. The reason Rexanna had come home to Wallace. Her aunt Trixie excepted.

"I didn't want to read it, at first," she added.

"But now you do." He almost snarled the challenge.

"I didn't know you then." She took a step toward him. And stopped.

He had a crazy need to hold her. To feel her against him. He needed her comfort, the assurance that she didn't think he was the monster everyone else did.

Correction. Not everyone. Cord and Harrie. Her uncle Charlie. The whole Wallace community. They'd given him a new chance. A place to start over.

Acceptance.

He wanted to put Rexanna in their circle. He wanted her to believe him. He wanted her to hate the lies as much as he did.

She meant that much to him.

His fists clenched. He dredged up the ugly memories. He had to tell the story one more time. For her sake. For his own.

"Doreen was in my last movie. She had a thing for me. Didn't matter that she was married. She played with every man in every movie she was in. I wasn't the only one."

Rexanna eyed him. "Why would her husband put up with it?"

"She paid the bills. Gave him a comfortable life." Roan kept talking. He still hadn't moved from the table. Rexanna hadn't moved far from the sink. The two of them, sharing the ugliness of his story. "She was under contract to the studio. Seven years. She wanted more from them. The lead role in my father's new movie, specifically. She was good enough, but they wouldn't commit to giving it to her."

"Why did she stay?"

"The studio controlled everyone. The hours we worked. How we lived. Who we associated with. The harder we worked, the more money they made. We were their property, to be used at their whim."

Rexanna made a small sound of commiseration. Roan didn't want her pity. He just wanted her to know the truth.

"Doreen took up drinking and drugs. One night, she called me. Said she was sick and needed to go to the hospital. Her husband was out of town. Like a fool, I believed her. She was crying hysterically over the phone, so I dropped everything and went to her house."

He glanced away. He'd been a stupid idiot for falling for her manipulation. To this day, this moment, it cut through him, making him bleed inside.

"Some actresses made crying an art form. Doreen was one of them. As soon as I got there, I knew she wasn't sick but drunk. She'd taken some pills, too. I found them in the kitchen, next to a bottle of bourbon." He met Rexanna's somber gaze. "I put her to bed and left. Figured she'd just sleep it off, and she'd be better by the time her husband came home."

Rexanna nodded, as if she agreed the plan had been sound.

"I found out later he wasn't out of town at all, but at his favorite club. Poker Night." More stupidity. More manipulation. "When he came home, he found her at the bottom of the stairs. She claimed I came over and made some advances she didn't want, then pushed her in a fit of rage. He believed her."

The pain still burned through Roan. Probably always would.

"That's when the studio got involved. They were all in on the deal. Scandal meant free publicity. The movie we were in had finished filming. Next step was promoting it, so the studio fed the story to the *Scoop*, pictures and all."

Rexanna's fingers flew to her mouth. "Oh, Roan."

"Doreen's husband wanted to file charges against me to make the scandal even bigger, but my father stepped in to prevent it. The studio had the police in their pocket. The charges went nowhere. But I was ruined. I was done in Hollywood. Literally and figuratively."

Her eyes welled. "I was no better. I believed the gossip. I—oh, I'm sorry."

She moved toward him, and his arms opened, taking her body to his, holding her tight against him. Her arms circled his back. Her forehead sank against his shoulder.

He soaked in her warmth. Her solace and compassion. She gave him what he craved most.

Her strength.

"My father sent the studio's fixer to get me out of town. I hated him for it. I felt like he'd abandoned me as his son." Roan's jaw pressed into her hair, and his belly churned from the memory. "It was your great-aunt Adelaide who suggested the T Bar M. She made arrangements with Cord to set me up with a job. The fixer made sure I showed up to take it."

Rexanna drew back. "A fixer?"

"He works for the studio. Fixes their problems. In my case, they wanted to protect Doreen's addictions and keep her working for them for the rest of her contract. I, on the other hand, had finished my contract. I was expendable. There were hundreds more actors ready to take my place. I might've been Sergio Bertoletti's son, but I wasn't their money-maker. She was the bigger name. The bigger talent."

"How unfair to you," she whispered.

"Didn't matter." He drew his thumb across her lower lip.

"The gossip columnists should be ashamed of themselves for printing such a story."

A corner of his mouth lifted. Funny how she made it easier to talk about it and help him get through the pain.

"Doreen had the injuries. Not me. Made for an easy story to tell."

"I feel awful for what you've been through. If only—"

"No 'if only', Rexanna." His voice roughened. "If the scandal hadn't happened, then I wouldn't have come to the T Bar M. This ranch saved my sanity. Your family... they've made me a part of them. You know how lucky you are to have them?"

Again, her eyes welled, and her throat worked, and Roan didn't want her to cry on his account.

Something moved inside his chest, an emotion he could barely define as nebulous as it was, and if she intended to agree with him, or even if she didn't, he stole the opportunity by lowering his head and taking her mouth to his.

An unexpected desperation swept through him. The realization she would always have her home to come back to. Her family would be here, a part of her, but what about him? What did he have, after all he'd lost? How long would she be here to share it with him? Not long. Not nearly long enough. She had her own life, a different life, experiencing parts of the world he likely never would.

His arms encircled her even closer, seizing these moments and making them forever his. His head angled, deepening the kiss. The passion of it. She melded into him, giving him what he wanted, needed, as if she needed him just as much. He tasted her sweetness, soaked in her warmth, her allure and femininity, and just as she made him want more than he should, a persistent dinging tore into his awareness.

The oven's timer.

She drew back slowly, and her lashes lifted. "Well." Her expression softened in wry amusement. "Looks like the Jell-O is ready."

9

Supper could wait.

After Rexanna added shredded carrots and chopped celery to the Jell-O and stirred them together, she returned the salad to the refrigerator for its final jelling. Once the chicken had finished roasting and cooled enough to debone, she piled the pieces into another pan, covered the meat and juices with aluminum foil, and added that to the refrigerator, too.

Chicken would heat up just fine, and she'd much rather go riding with Roan.

He'd made fast friends with Mack while she finished up her cooking and rushed through a cleanup, grabbed her hat from the bedroom, then headed for the living room for her Weatherby. One of her grandfather's most emphatic rules was never to ride the range unarmed. No telling what they could encounter, anything from a rattlesnake to a cougar or something just as dangerous on two legs. Rexanna, like everyone else on the ranch, made sure to comply, and she took the rifle from the rack.

Yet the mahogany case on the mantel drew her, an indiscernible pull that defied Roan waiting outside. She couldn't figure it, this pull, but she gave in to the need to see the pink pistol again, and gently, she lifted the lid.

There it was, still lying against the green velvet. The mother-of-pearl handle seemed to twinkle in the room's afternoon light, and with her free hand, she lifted the little revolver from its resting place.

Odd how it warmed her palm even though the gun case itself was cooler to the touch, reminding her of another warmth. Roan's... whose body had enveloped hers with a delicious heat. Strong and solid, he'd smelled of the wind, of horse and leather and pure man.

And his kisses, oh, had she ever been affected more? Their mastery, their tenderness had consumed her every thought, her every sensation, rocking her off-balance. She'd had to cling to him to keep from sinking, as if she'd fallen into quicksand. He'd consumed her with those kisses, and if she wasn't careful....

Well, things had changed between them, for sure. Somehow. It wasn't so long ago she would've callously attributed his masculine appeal to his reputation. A man with looks that could make a woman swoon. An actor who could manipulate her attraction to him.

But she'd believed his story. Every word he spoke about the injustices done to him from so many. Their betrayals had torn at her heart. His pain had been real.

Pensive, taking more time to ponder than she should, she stroked the pink grip with her thumb.

Had she fallen for the pistol's legend? Was she beginning to believe its promise?

She couldn't know for sure.

Sighing, she returned the pink pistol to its case and shut the lid, giving it a thoughtful pat before she turned and headed to the porch, pulling the door shut behind her. A slight breeze tugged at Aunt Trixie's hanging things, and Rexanna tilted her head back, watching them sway from the porch ceiling.

"I have a friend who owns an art gallery." Roan strode toward her, Mack on his heels. "He might be interested in taking them."

She glanced at him in surprise. "Really?"

"Can't keep letting the little birdies hang out in the open. Weather's hard on them."

"Yes," she murmured, studying them again. "They're pretty, in their own way."

"Trixie thought so." A corner of his mouth lifted.

"Well, I'll have to do something, I suppose." She descended the stairs, meeting him at the bottom. Again, she tilted her head back, this time to see him better. Or was it to allow herself to be captured by those inky black eyes of his, framed by dark lashes? "I like the idea of putting them in a gallery."

"Lots of artistic-minded folks would enjoy them."

"Exactly. Out here, no one would after I—"

Leave.

The word stuck in her throat.

A cloud seemed to cross his features, and a long moment passed, punctuated by her inability to say what they both knew. What she never intended to hide.

His expression grim, he stepped back, indicating the mare tethered next to his buckskin.

"Speaking of enjoying, thought you'd like to ride this pretty little filly," he said gruffly.

Rexanna shook off her own cloud before it rained on her time with Roan. What little she had left, anyway. She rounded Roan's horse with renewed interest for the younger one.

"She's beautiful," she said, stroking the long neck. "What's her name?"

"Cream Puff. Harrie named her for her color. Calls her Puff, though."

"The name fits." Rexanna slid the Weatherby into the scabbard on the saddle and crooned introductions with more long rubs against the sleek hide, admiring her docile nature. The mare would be a pleasure to ride.

"She's foaled from Dandelion," he said, untying the reins from the porch post.

Rexanna's eyes widened. The yellow dun had been her first horse, and she'd named her with a girlish perspective. "She is? I knew she had a baby, but Grandma never said much."

"Maybe because you never asked." He strode closer. "Mount up."

She ignored the barb and changed sides with the horse. She deserved the sting, because he was right. She hadn't.

"Dandelion is twenty-one years old now." He handed her the reins. "Fighting arthritis. No one rides her anymore, or else I would've brought her out."

He knew more about the animals on her family's ranch than she did, and why should that bother her? Making her feel like a stranger in her own home?

"I'll be sure to go see her," Rexanna murmured.

"Bet she'd like that." He grinned. "I would, if I was her."

He swung into the saddle with an agile grace, as if he'd been born to ride a horse. Settling in, creaking leather, he took the reins and guided the buckskin away from the cabin and around her pickup, parked in the drive.

Telling Mack to stay close, Rexanna joined him, and they began an easy walk toward the corral. A pair of alpaca heads appeared from inside the barn, and it wasn't long before the third one showed up, looking so big-eyed and curious that Rexanna couldn't help but laugh.

"They're so darned cute," she said, not for the first time. She drew up next to the fence and reached over to pet each woolly head. "It's hard not to get attached to them. They're like little people with separate personalities."

Roan crossed his wrists over the saddle horn. "You remembered to feed them this morning, right?"

She tossed him an exasperated look. "Yes, Roan. I remembered to feed them."

He shrugged. "Sorry. Just checking."

"And I cleaned out their stalls, raked up their scat inside the corral, and gave them plenty of water, too."

Looking properly apologetic, he leaned from the saddle, took her hand, and dropped a kiss onto her knuckles. "Sorry. Didn't mean to insult you."

How could she stay annoyed when he charmed her

with his gallantry? "You didn't." She took the reins again, the feel of his lips still on her skin. "I've been gone a long time. It's easy for you—or anyone else—to think I'm out of practice with ranch stock."

"Won't happen again."

She wanted to hug him. "It's okay. I'll forgive you if it does. Where shall we go next?"

"Want to see my place?"

"Sure."

Their mounts fell into a lazy walk as they left the corral behind and headed into open country. She relaxed in the saddle, allowing her body to move with the mare's gait. Lush prairie grass blanketed the fields, and T Bar M cattle grazed in the distance, their hides little dots of color on the horizon. Her heart squeezed at the sight.

She hadn't taken the time to appreciate any of it for too long, and the immensity of what she had, of what she'd always taken for granted, burned through her.

Brennan land. Her family's ranch. Her heritage, most of all.

"About time for the alpacas to be shorn," Roan said, his tone conversational.

She shifted her thoughts. "They're pretty woolly, yes."

"It'd be real easy to make a little business out of it."

Her glance swiveled toward him. "From their wool, you mean?"

He, on the other hand, kept his gaze straightforward, one dark eye narrowed, as if his thinking consumed him. "Lots you can make with it. Scarves and shawls. Hats, socks, stuff like that."

Was he just making conversation?

"Yes," she said slowly. Uncertain.

"Their yarn is popular, too. Can be dyed in different colors. Women open shops, just to sell alpaca products."

"You make it sound easy, Roan. Shearing the wool is one thing. Selling it as a finished product is another. There's lots you have to do in between to make the fibers usable."

"Yep. I know." Finally, his shadowed gaze landed on her. "There's a processor in Kansas City who will clean and comb the yarn. Some folks do it themselves, even. But we could truck it in, then pick up the wool when it's ready."

"We." She frowned.

"Wouldn't be hard to do."

"With only three alpacas?" Her brow lifted.

"We'd have to increase the herd. That wouldn't be hard to do, either."

"Roan." There was that *we* word again, and her heart pumped a little faster. "Why are you telling me all this? None of it has anything to do with me."

"The herd is yours. What're you going to do with it?"

She stiffened from his challenge. "You've put a lot of thought into this, haven't you?"

"For a while now."

"Then maybe...." Her voice drifted off, and she exhaled.

What could she say? That since he was the one thinking about the alpacas so much, that he should take over the herd himself? Put into place all the ideas he'd just mentioned?

"Just think on it, Rexanna."

Think on making a business from alpaca wool when she already had her outfitting business, guiding hunters on wild game excursions? Doing so would bring her back to the T Bar M for good. A new commitment that couldn't include wild game hunting in even the most remote way.

The questions banged inside her head like balls on a pool table, punctuating her frustration. He'd smoothly upended her tidy world and the future she'd worked hard to build. Her plans. Her livelihood.

None of which pertained to the T Bar M.

Unexpected emotion stung the back of her eyes. She didn't want to be so torn. Up until now, her life had been perfectly planned and comfortable.

"Here we go," he said. "My humble abode."

Just like that, he switched the course of their conversation from one thing to another, leaving Rexanna practically dizzy. She forced herself to bank her frustration and focus on the rustic cabin made of mud-chinked logs in front of her. If he could talk about something different, so could she.

"I expected it to be in worse shape," she said, scanning the swept porch and sloped roof. "New shingles?"

"And a whole lot more, besides." He reined in, studying the structure, too. "Cord wouldn't let me pay him for rent. Said if I fixed the place up, that would be good enough for him. With Charlie's help, we put in new windows, new plumbing, new wiring."

His efforts were impressive. He'd even added a simple carport on one side to protect his Chrysler sedan from Kansas weather. The care he'd given to the old line camp would double its lifetime.

"Your place looks wonderful, Roan. A whole lot different than what you were used to in California, I'd warrant," she said.

"Like night and day. My apartment had more comforts, but this cabin has felt more like home than city living ever did."

"Why do you suppose that is?" she mused, her gaze trailing over the trampled grass along one side. She nudged the mare closer.

"Guess I'm just a country boy at heart." He paused. "What are you looking at?"

Tracking was a skill she'd learned years ago. She knew what prints belonged to which animal and the approximate time they were made. She could follow broken branches and markings on tree bark. But crumpled grass beneath a single window was something no animal she knew about would make.

Unless it was the two-legged kind.

"Do you ever peep inside your own window, Roan?" she murmured, skimming a keen glance over the sprawling rangeland beyond the cabin.

"Can't say as I have," he drawled. He studied the small section of ground, too. "Looks like someone beat me to it, though." He rubbed his jaw. "Can't imagine who."

"A photographer from California, I'd guess."

He shot her a sharp look. "How would you know that?"

"I met him in town this morning. A guy by the name of Kelly."

Roan reached into his saddlebag and pulled out binoculars. "Didn't happen to be driving a red-topped station wagon, did he?"

"He did, indeed." She dismounted and patted her thigh. "Come here, Mack."

The coonhound's ears pricked, and he abandoned his investigation of something off the path to follow Rexanna's direction. Pressing his nose into the trampled grass, his sleek body quivered in excitement. If there was a smell to be had, Mack would find it.

"Go, boy!" she commanded.

He whirled away from the cabin and took off across the field. Rexanna mounted up. She withdrew the Weatherby from the scabbard and took the reins.

"Maybe we'll get lucky, and the bum is out there somewhere," she said.

Roan lowered the lenses. "My guess is he will be. If not, he'll keep coming back until he gets what he wants from me."

Pictures, she knew. The inside scoop for whatever story he wanted to break for the papers and his own gain.

For Roan's sake, he needed to be stopped.

The horses cantered away from the cabin. Mack disappeared in a tree line, and her senses sharpened to detect some sign of him or to hear his baying howl. But except for the staccato of their horses' hooves against the packed ground, she saw nothing, heard nothing,

"You worried about losing Mack out here?" Roan asked.

"No. He'll come back if he doesn't find anything. If he does find what he's looking for, then he'll stay with his quarry until I get there."

"Smart dog," he muttered.

"The best."

Howling erupted, high-pitched and frenzied. As they rode closer, a slash of red appeared through the trees, and then, not unexpectedly, Mack's barking suddenly ended.

Rexanna's blood pumped in victory. He'd found what he was hunting for.

10

Roan switched the binoculars for his Remington rifle. Whoever was in that tree line needed a lesson in good manners, T Bar M style.

"Shall we give him a little scare?" he asked in a low voice.

"He's got one coming."

"I like the way you think."

"You learn fast, cowboy."

Side by side, their horses broke into the tree line, and Mack's growls sounded more persistent the closer they got. Vicious, even, though Roan knew the coonhound was a pussycat at heart.

A man in a gray fedora and suit stood next to the red-topped station wagon with one leg extended, trying to shake off Mack's grip on his trousers while holding onto the door handle for balance. A camera lay on the hood, looking as if it had been dropped there in a hurry.

Not even the approach of two armed riders on horses distracted him from his desperate attempt to free himself. Gave Roan some grim pleasure, seeing his fear. He had it coming, for sure.

He darted them both a furtive look. "Hey, lady! Call off your mutt, will you?"

Rexanna, cool as ice, halted. "He's as far from a mutt as he can get. Real smart, too. I'd show him a little more respect, if I were you."

"If he bites me, I'll sue you for everything you've got."

"He won't bite unless I tell him to." She kept the butt of the Weatherby pressed against her shoulder. "Off, Mack. Come."

Immediately, her dog obeyed and released his grip, trotting quickly toward the mare before sitting, his body tensed and ready for any new command Rexanna might give him. The photographer straightened and gave his leg a little shake, as if he was glad he still had possession of it.

"Did you forget I warned you about trespassers?" Rexanna asked.

He scowled and tipped his fedora higher on his forehead. "What's the big deal about ranchers and trespassers around here, anyway? Plenty of room for everyone. This place is so big, no one even saw me."

Roan was done with his excuses. Time to play his

hunch. "Didn't need to see you to know you were at my place, looking in the window. Some folks would say that was a crime that needs reporting."

Nonplussed, the photographer's gaze swung to him, and his expression brightened. "Figured that's where you were staying these days, Roan. You playing a real live cowboy now?"

Roan kept the Remington leveled and aimed. His finger itched to pull the trigger, but civility and his own sanity kept him from it. Kept him hanging on tight to his temper, too. "Depends on who wants to know. You writing a story for one of the trades?"

"Your fans are wondering about you." The man's smile could have charmed the leaves off the trees, inspiring anyone to tell him what he wanted to know.

And inspired, Roan wasn't.

His lip curled. "I'll bet they are."

"It's true." His arm lifted, imitating a make-believe headline in the air. *"Disgraced Hollywood Actor Starts New Life as Cowboy."* Looking pleased with his own idea, he lowered his arm. "Guaranteed to sell. We might even pay you for the story. I could look into it, if you want."

"Get out," Roan growled.

"Fans will love knowing you've moved on from Doreen Adams and have a new woman in your life. An heiress to the T Bar M Ranch, no less." As if Roan hadn't spoken, he again fashioned a headline. *"Grieving Wild Game Hunter Falls for Roan Bertoletti,* and then I could go into how one of her clients was mauled to death by a wild bear—"

Rexanna emitted a horrified cry. Her finger moved over the trigger, and the photographer's fedora flipped into the air, landing several yards away.

He yelped and jumped back, holding up both hands, the color gone from his face. "Hey! Hey! That was close! Don't shoot anymore, okay?"

"How do you know about me?" Rexanna grated. "Who told you?"

"One of the waitresses at Mama Jane's. The place with the free slice of pie, remember? The Brennans are a prominent family around here, with their big ranch and all. She had a lot to tell." He talked fast, as if his life depended on it. And given Rexanna's hurt and skill with a rifle, it probably did. "Word got out about what happened in Alaska, and that's why you came back, so I did a little digging and got the whole scoop. I'll just be reporting what everyone else around here already knows." He choked out a laugh. "Small town gossip and all that, right?"

"We might be small, but we protect our own." Roan lowered the Remington, swung a leg over the pommel, and slid out of the saddle. With the stealth of a cougar, he approached the red-topped station wagon and the man standing beside it. "What's your name?"

The scrawny throat above the shirt collar moved. "I'm not telling you."

"You think it won't be hard to find out about a lowlife reporter wanting to write about Sergio Bertoletti's son?"

"It's Kelly, okay? *Kelly.*"

"Who are you reporting for?"

"Confidential, Roan. You know how an inside scoop works, right? Everything has to be kept under wraps."

"I have plenty of friends in LA who can help me

find out." Roan set the Remington on the tan hood and took the camera in both hands.

"Hey, leave that alone!" Kelly yelped.

Roan found the compartment holding the film, opened it, and pulled out the roll. Leaving the compartment open, he returned the camera to the hood with a clatter and dropped the film into his shirt pocket.

"Time for you to leave, bum." Roan opened the automobile's door.

"Give me my film back!"

"Not going to happen."

"C'mon, Roan." His voice turned pleading. "Never thought you'd be one to steal someone else's property. You want me to press charges? Give you more bad publicity?"

Roan grasped him by the lapel of his coat. Hard. Kelly stumbled forward, and Roan gave him some help getting behind the wheel. He took the filmless camera off the hood, snatched the fedora off the ground, and tossed both into Kelly's lap. Roan shut the station wagon's door, loud enough to let the photographer know he was on the brink of losing his law-abiding manners.

"If I find out you wrote even one word about Miss Brennan, or her family's ranch, or me, I'll see that you're ruined for every newspaper or magazine in the country." He took the Remington and aimed the barrel at the open driver's window. "Don't make me say it again. Get off this land, and don't come back."

"Look." Kelly ran his tongue over his lower lip; sweat left a sheen on his forehead. "Can we talk about this? I mean, I really need—"

Roan fired into the ground, inches from the station

wagon's front tire. Dirt flew into the air and pinged against the tan door.

Kelly spat a curse, revved the engine and, grinding gears, he tore off down the path and past the tree line, fishtailing over the thick grass.

Roan kept watch to make sure the red-top disappeared. When it did, he turned back toward Rexanna. She kept her attention on returning the Weatherby to the scabbard, but her silence told him everything he needed to know.

He approached her with a gesture to dismount. "Come here."

He expected her to question the request. Another time, she might have, but she complied, leaving the saddle with the grace so much a part of her. Might be she needed him to be a little closer than what she could be, sitting on a horse. She stood in front of him, her blonde head tilted.

"Thank you," she murmured.

"You okay?" he asked quietly.

"Not really." She glanced away. "He was just crass, you know? About Annie, I mean."

The dismay in her voice reached inside his chest and squeezed. Still holding his Remington, he hooked his free arm around her neck and pulled her against him. When her hat got in the way, she took it off, and he took advantage to place his palm against the back of her head, keeping her against his shoulder.

"Reporters like him are a different breed. They'll do anything to get their story. Bylines are their claim to fame," he said into her hair.

"They're heartless."

"Worse." Her warmth seeped into him. Her

womanly shape, too. "They don't care whose privacy they destroy or expose. It's all about them." He exhaled. "He hurt you because of me, Rexanna. It's my fault he brought you into a scandal you had nothing to do with."

"No, Roan. Not your fault at all." She appealed to him, her eyes deep red-brown pools of pain. Regret, too, like his own. "Annie's death is a tragedy I'll always have to live with. People will never forget." She hesitated. "And like you with Doreen, what happened with Annie was out of my control."

He didn't have all the details. He wasn't sure how much Harrie and Cord knew, either. But when Rexanna was ready to talk, he'd listen.

Given the pain showing in her pretty face, now might be the time.

"Annie went off on her own when we were on an Alaskan excursion. She disobeyed my orders to stay put until I could go up the mountain with her. But she wanted her bear, and she made all kinds of mistakes to get it. Unfortunately, the bear got her, instead." Rexanna emitted a quavery sigh, and Roan's gut twisted. From her words. From her anguish. "Her father was a rich executive for a regional airline in California. Her death made the papers. It's not surprising that someone in Kansas would catch wind of it. Lots of folks here in Wallace get their news from bigger cities."

"Really tough what happened."

"You have no idea."

"I think I do."

"I thought coming home for a little while would help me escape. I'd hoped it would put me in my own little bubble on the ranch and keep me safe from the outside world and all the memories. From the talk." Her forehead eased back onto his shoulder. He palmed her spine, slowly, over and over. "I was wrong. Annie's death will always stay with me. And sometimes...."

She took so long to finish, Roan lowered his jaw into her hair. "Sometimes what, Rexi?"

She exhaled into his shirt. "I think I should quit. Never hunt wildlife again."

He stilled. He hadn't expected her to say that. Not even close. Hunting big game was who she was... what she'd been for her adult life. And yet....

He couldn't deny the hope that fluttered in his veins. He had no right to want her to give up her business. To stay on the T Bar M. But the hope flickered and flared of its own accord, latched onto his heart, and wouldn't let go....

"You're feeling pretty low right now," he murmured. "Easy to want to give up. But things happen, Rexanna, and—"

Her head came up, and tears shimmered beneath her lashes. "A young woman died on my account, Roan," she grated. "She was my responsibility. No one else's. Her parents paid me good money to bring them to Alaska and get them home again. They *trusted* me in that."

"Like I trusted Doreen to stay in bed and sleep off the alcohol?" he shot back, sharper than he intended. "I left her in good faith. I expected her to do what she told me she'd do. Stay put and sleep. But she didn't do either of those things." His jaw tightened. How could he make Rexanna understand? How could he take away the hurt that was torturing her, right here in his arms? "You're innocent of Annie's decision, Rexanna. Just like I'm innocent of anything Doreen did after I left her house. Her decision was her own. So was Annie's. It's not fair to you or to me, but unfairness happens in this life, and we're both paying the price."

"Yes." Her chin quivered. "We are."

He slid his fingers into her hair, gently pushing the silken weight off the side of her face. She needed to tighten her barrette, but until she did, he intended to enjoy the feel of touching the blonde strands. Touching her, too.

"So, what are we going to do about it?" he murmured. "Make ourselves miserable by feeling sorry for ourselves? Will that change the past?"

She peered up at him, moisture clinging to her lashes. "If only."

"It won't. We have to move on. Become a better person for it."

"You make it sound easy, Roan. It's not."

"Never said it was easy. I wallowed in my share of self-pity when I came here, believe me. Pretty much drowned in it, in fact. But it didn't take long for me to realize that if it wasn't for Doreen, I wouldn't be living on the T Bar M. And if I wasn't living on the T Bar M, I wouldn't be holding you right now. Which makes everything she put me through worth it." His head lowered, and his need to take her mouth to his overrode any words he could think of to convince her. "*Worth it.*"

Her breath caught. Her head tilted, her eyes drifted closed, and she met him coming with a need that fueled his own. The delicious softness of her lips formed an instant addiction that tilted him sideways and sent him tumbling into the sensation of her sweet womanliness.

She kept him breathing. Existing. Already, she filled his life in ways no other had done before her, enriching his world. Strengthening his purpose.

His embrace tightened. If he could meld her skin with his to make her part of him forever, he would. He refused to think of her leaving him, the ranch, and returning to her life in the wild.

He could only think of her now. Like this. The two of them with their bodies pressed together, mouths clinging, hearts pumping as one.

It took every shred of his sanity to end the kiss, his reluctance turning as palpable as hers. He could almost fall into those pretty eyes and never come out.

"You're very convincing, cowboy. You know that?" she said, her voice a sultry whisper.

"Yeah? Well, if you need more convincing, just let me know. I'm happy to oblige."

She laughed softly and drew away, and the afternoon air cooled his chest through his shirt, chasing the warmth she'd given him.

"Suppose we'll see Kelly again?" she asked.

"Not if he knows what's good for him. Which he does now, thanks to you." He chucked her under the chin. "That was quite a shot, you know. Through his hat."

She shrugged. "He made a worthy target. He had the scare coming."

Roan grunted. "Always heard you were good."

"Runs in the family. My great-grandfather was a notorious outlaw. Ambidextrous, too."

"Seriously?"

"His name was Slick-Shot Billy Hayes."

Intrigued, he grinned. "Sounds like someone from

the Old West."

"Because he was."

Had a woman fascinated him more? "You must've inherited your shooting abilities from him."

"I prefer to think I inherited them from my grandmother. She was a great shot, too."

"Still is." The one time he'd shot pheasant with her and Cord had been eye-opening. She could pick them out of the sky left and right. Never missed. "She's an amazing woman."

Movement out of the corner of his eye stole his attention off Rexanna and toward her coonhound, investigating something in the grass with his nose pressed to the ground, tail wagging.

Rexanna, too, noticed he'd taken off on his own without the photographer to keep him interested, and she slid a sharp whistle through her teeth. Mack gave up his curiosity and moseyed back to her side. She stepped closer to the mare and lifted her foot into the stirrup, mounting up with ease. "It's getting late, Roan. We'd best go if we want a good ride before dark."

But his priorities had shifted, and she was right. Time was ticking.

"I'll have to give you a raincheck." He mounted, too. "Hope you don't mind. There's something I have to do first."

With a little luck, he might catch his father still at the office.

11

Tension bristled through Roan. Even after all these months, it was still there.

He hadn't called his father since he left Los Angeles. If it wasn't for that bum photographer, Roan wouldn't be calling him now. But he had to step over the ugly memories like they were poisoned mud puddles and find solid ground. He had to take the risk that even after kicking him out of town, his father might refuse to speak to him. If he did give Roan the time, well, he'd have to shut up for a change and let Roan do the talking.

His father's no-nonsense-and-utterly efficient secretary, Margaret, sounded happy to hear from him. Surprised, too. The two-hour time difference between California and Kansas had worked in his favor. Margaret assured him his father was at his desk, and she'd put him on the line as soon as she could, and would he mind waiting on hold while she made sure he took the call?

Roan sat on Rexanna's couch with his elbows braced on his knees and the telephone receiver pressed to his ear. Waiting. Enduring the tension.

Thanks to Harrie and Cord, who had paid extra to have a private line on the ranch, at least an operator wouldn't be listening in, sparing Roan the gossip. Rexanna had been quick to allow him the use of her phone since his place didn't have one, and he was thankful for that, too.

He could hear her moving about in the kitchen, warming the roasted and deboned chicken in the oven, boiling potatoes on the stove, and setting plates and silverware on the table. Preparing for their supper together. Giving him privacy. Not that he had anything to hide from her. She knew as much as anyone what had happened with Doreen, and Roan had no secrets to keep.

"Roan." Sergio Bertoletti's cultured voice, faintly accented in Italian, broke through the line and yanked Roan back to the present. "How are you, son?"

Son.

Roan almost sneered the word out loud. What father used a hired man to boot his only child out of his career, order him out of the state and halfway across the country, with no consideration of what said child may or may not have done, all for the purpose of keeping up appearances for the studio he worked for?

"Good." Roan spoke the word with a terse snap but conceded the question sounded genuine, surprisingly enough. "I need you to do something for me."

"You got troubles?"

"Unfortunately."

"Then name it."

Roan's grip tightened on the telephone receiver. He never thought his father would refuse, but the smooth agreement was like an unexpected flame to dry tinder, banked for too long and ready to flare. "That easy, Dad?" He couldn't hold back his bitterness. "When you couldn't even step in to protect my job or my reputation because yours was more important? Like the studio's?"

"You think I wouldn't have done things differently if I could?"

"You tell me."

"You had too much evidence against you. My hands were tied."

"I could have been charged with a crime I didn't commit. A conviction would have been on my record for the rest of my life."

"Doreen's husband had dollar signs in his eyes. He wanted to sue you for everything you had. I kept him from it, and the charges never happened. Give me credit for at least that."

Roan's eyes closed on a wave of pain. Of regret. He dredged up the fairness his father deserved.

"I do," he muttered. Yet, the agony of what he'd endured since then at the hands of a spoiled brat of an actress refused to go away. "Since when did anyone believe anything Doreen Adams ever said? She's a fraud, and so are those pictures."

"I know." His father's voice lowered, sounding tired. "They were staged, and she only admitted it after she got the lead part in my new Western coming out next year. As soon as the ink dried on the contract, she admitted she worked with a friend of hers who's a columnist for the *Scoop*. Together, they arranged to have a photographer take photos of her injuries and get them published. Mannix used one of the studio doctors to confirm her allegations that she was pushed."

"Just like that."

"Afraid so."

"You gave her the lead, didn't you?"

"I recommended her for it, yes."

"Why?" Roan gritted. "After what she'd done?"

"To shut her up, that's why," his father shot back. "Shirley secretly taped Doreen's admission, and I threatened to expose the truth if she ever so much as spoke your name again. She got what she wanted. She was only too happy to agree."

Sighing heavily, Roan removed his hat, tossed it on the coffee table, and raked a hand through his hair. Had he really lived that life for so many years? How had he survived the craziness? The dysfunction?

"Whether or not you agree, Roan," Sergio said, "I made sure Mannix got you out of town to save you from the cesspool you were living in. What *I'm* still living in. You had too much integrity to fit in with the movie star crowd. You were always more like your mother."

Emotion pushed up through Roan's chest. "I'll take that as a compliment."

"It was intended as one."

"I wanted you to be proud of me when I went out there. I had big shoes to fill. I was expected to be a younger version of you. Your success. Your reputation."

"I know, son." Roan couldn't deny the remorse sailing through the phone line. "It was impossible for you to be something you weren't. Unbelievably unfair, too, though neither of us could change it at the time. But you were young, too young to be on your own. As your father, I had the responsibility to take care of you after your mom died. Los Angeles wasn't ideal, but it was all I could offer you."

Rexanna appeared beneath the archway separating the living room from the kitchen. She held up a bottle of Blatz beer, her brow raised in question.

He nodded. Her timing couldn't have been better.

She headed back into the kitchen. A drawer opened. The bottle cap fizzed. In the next moment, so did another.

"It's past us now, Roan. It was a tough way for you to make the break from that kind of life. You were a fine actor, for what it's worth. But you're done. You've moved on."

"Not quite."

Rexanna entered the living room, a bottle of beer in each hand. Roan straightened and accepted the bottle she offered, then lifted his arm in silent invitation to join him on the couch. She complied and sat, her thigh next to his.

"A guy showed up here," Roan continued, giving his father his attention again. Wasn't easy when he'd rather put all his attention on Rexanna instead. "Drove all over the ranch looking for me. Turns out he's a photographer wanting to do a story. A follow-up after what happened in LA."

"Does he work for one of the trades?"

"Yes. He wouldn't tell me which one." He stole a quick swallow of Blatz, then lowered the bottle. "Not only is he trespassing, he intends to involve a member of the Brennan family. I want him stopped. I want his story canned before he even gets started."

"I'll see what I can do."

"Get Mannix on it." Roan rarely told his father what to do, but he'd learned firsthand how unscrupulous the fixer could be. "The photographer's name is Kelly. Don't know his last name. Drives a red-topped station wagon. Chevrolet One-Fifty."

A moment passed, most likely the time his father took to jot a few notes. Roan took another swallow of cold brew.

"Anything else?" Sergio asked, on the line again.

Roan pulled up the automobile's license number in his mind, the combination of letters and numbers in yellow on black that he'd memorized, and relayed the information. "He had a '55 validation tab. Looked like he was paid up and legit." He smirked. "The studio's police will appreciate you making their job easier."

"Mannix, too."

"Exactly."

Sergio hesitated. "One last question."

Roan was out of information but shrugged. "Sure."

"Are you happy, son?"

He stilled at the query. Happy? Safe? Satisfied? Right where he wanted to be?

Yes. All those things. He dropped his beer-holding arm around Rexanna's shoulders and pulled her closer.

"Very," he said in a low voice.

"Good." A gust of breath rushed through the phone. "I've called, you know. I don't want you to think I haven't tried, but... Harrie said it was too soon."

"Did she?" The woman's instincts touched him. Her compassion, too. He couldn't find her interference unacceptable. "She was right."

"Adelaide has been wanting to come for a visit. Hated missing Trixie's funeral, you know. Would it... be all right if I came with her?"

Roan's heart squeezed. Had he ever known the famous and debonair Sergio Bertoletti to be unsure of himself? Or this humbled?

A great weight lifted off Roan's shoulders. All the resentment, the uncertainties of his father's intentions, fled. Almost miraculous how much better it was just saying the words someone needed to hear. The truth, worth its weight in gold.

"I'd like that, Dad."

"We'll plan on it, then. I'll be in touch about the photographer."

Sounding like he had a smile in his voice, his father hung up, and Roan dropped the receiver into the cradle. He leaned back against the couch cushions, and Rexanna relaxed against him.

"Everything go okay with your dad?" she asked.

"Better than expected."

"Wow. That's good."

"He wants to come to the ranch. I'd like him to meet you, Rexanna."

She blinked and went still. "Roan." She drew away and sat straighter. "When is he coming? I mean, there isn't time. I can't..."

His senses coiled. "Can't what? Meet him?"

"You know I can't." She stood so abruptly, the beer swished in her bottle. "You *know* I have to leave in a few days."

He stood, too. Slower. "Only because you want to."

"Want to?" She huffed. "I have a business. I have responsibilities to clients who have paid me money to take them hunting. Do you expect me to just—just ignore them? Pretend I don't know them? Walk away as if I'd never signed a contract with them?"

"You the only wild game hunter around?"

"No." Her throat moved. "But I'm *their* wild game hunter."

He was sinking fast and on his way to ruining the evening when their time together had been just about perfect. Their kisses, even more so.

But there was no turning back. Words needed to be said. Words she needed to hear. His logic, if never voiced, would only fester with worry and uncertainty and regret.

The truth. Worth its weight in gold.

He took a step toward her. She took a quick one back. He didn't move, then. His fist gripped the neck of his beer bottle.

"You ever take the time to think about your grandparents, Rexanna? You think they'll be around forever?"

Her breath quickened. "What do you mean? Are they sick?"

"They're fine, far as I know. But they're in their seventies. Running a ranch the size of the T Bar M is getting to be too much for them."

She stood frozen. "Uncle Charlie is here. He helps."

"Great-uncle, you mean. He's only a few years younger than they are. He and his wife never had kids. Adelaide never married. She never had kids, either. Neither will ever run the ranch."

Mute, as if her voice was stolen right out of her throat, she shook her head.

"Your parents, both gone." Roan spoke carefully. "That leaves you, Rexanna. You're the only one left in the Brennan family to take over the T Bar M. You ever think about that?"

"No. I mean, yes, I have. Of course, I have." She stood taller.

"It'll all be yours one day. The whole operation. You going to know what to do when it happens?"

"I really don't think my grandparents' affairs are any of your business, Roan," she said stiffly.

"Trixie's cabin is only the beginning. The first of your inheritance."

"They've never pressured me with any of this. Not one word."

"And take away the dream you worked years for? Your own business? On their account?" Might be she'd think he was the villain in this discussion, but it was a part he had to play. "No. They wouldn't." He paused. "They love you too much to do that."

Her eyes welled.

"Think about it, Rexi," he said quietly. Using her family's nickname came easy. Maybe too easy. "That's all I ask."

"I'll do that." She cleared her throat, and her composure returned. "I have to check the potatoes.

Excuse me."

She left him standing there, alone in the living room, keenly aware that for all his talking, not once had she said she wanted to stay.

12

The Next Morning

Rexanna rose on tiptoe to reach the top of the window with her wet rag, and with thorough left and right sweeps, she removed the dust and fine layer of Kansas dirt off the glass. After dropping the rag into a bucket of soapy water, she took a dry square of cotton toweling and repeated the process until the wet streaks were gone, and the window shone clean.

Finally, she was done. After washing the outside windows first, this was the last one left in the living room to wash on the inside. The sun streaming in brightened the whole space, showing off her efforts. No telling how long it'd been since Aunt Trixie had washed windows, but it'd been a while, given the dirt buildup. Grandma had mentioned the place needed deep cleaning, since Aunt Trixie hadn't been up to doing it herself, and she'd been right.

Her grandmother had always been here, a vital part of the T Bar M. She was strong. A hard worker. Nothing was too much for her to handle, especially if Grandpa was around to help.

But Rexanna was glad her grandmother hadn't taken on Trixie's heavy-duty housekeeping herself. Washing windows. At her age?

You ever take the time to think about your grandparents, Rexanna?

Roan's voice popped into her head, as vividly as if he were standing in front of her, and *oh, yes*, she wanted to tell Roan now. Because she'd been thinking of them the whole night long, thanks to him and his bold, no-nonsense challenges.

You think they'll be around forever?

The words pelted her like blowing sleet. Rexanna stood in the living room, bathed in warm sunlight and hardly noticing from the stubborn chill on her skin. They wouldn't live forever, and how awful would it be if they *died*, and she wasn't on the ranch to tell them goodbye? Because she was too far away on some wild game expedition, and she didn't get word in time? Or couldn't travel back in time....

...they're in their seventies...

Not terribly old, but not young, either. Who would care for them if they were hurt or sick? Like they'd cared for Aunt Trixie when she couldn't tend to herself, at least not properly?

The possibility that they wouldn't have anyone tore at Rexanna's heart. Oh, there'd be doctors and nurses. Friends from Wallace, too. They were loved by the whole community, but it wasn't the same as family.

She was their family. Rexanna Brennan. Their only grandchild.

Think about it, Rexi.

Rexanna emitted a miserable groan. She'd done all kinds of thinking, tossed and turned the whole night long over it, and nothing gave her answers. No comfortable ones, anyway. She strode into the kitchen and yanked open the cabinet door under the sink. She found a faded piece of flannel for dusting and an ancient-looking bottle of Old English polish.

Not that the cabin needed dusting again. Grandma had just done so before Rexanna arrived, but it wouldn't hurt to give the furniture another go, especially since work had always been an outlet to assuage her frustrations. Like a bee in its hive, she dusted the windowsills, the lamps, the end tables, and the coffee table where only last night, Roan had propped his booted feet while they listened to Jack Benny on the radio.

The blood quickened in her veins.

He'd stayed for dinner and wolfed down the chicken, potatoes, and her Jell-O salad, allowing her to discover there was some real pleasure in feeding a man who appreciated her cooking and didn't mind telling her so.

Like husbands and wives through the ages, she'd thought at the time, right there at the kitchen table, and she'd had to stop *that* thinking in a real hurry.

He'd regaled her with stories about life on a movie set, and actors and actresses she'd only heard about, but that he'd met personally. With his low voice and unassuming air, he made for a fascinating storyteller, and she could have listened to him forever.

"Noticed you had that poster of Frank Sinatra hanging on your bedroom wall," he'd said conversationally.

"It's been there since I was thirteen."

"Nice guy."

"My favorite singer. He beats out Elvis, in my mind. At least, sometimes. Elvis is cool, too, though."

"Rumor has it Frank's eyes aren't really blue."

Rexanna's fork halted halfway to her mouth. "What do you mean, they're not blue?"

"Contact lenses."

If she hadn't had her wits about her, she would have dropped the fork right onto her Jell-O salad.

But she couldn't stop her gasp of horror. "No!"

"It's true." He scooped up a big bite of potatoes and hauled them into his mouth, those dark eyes glittering with amusement.

She sat back in her chair like a deflated balloon. Did Frank have to fool his adoring public, too, like so many others in Hollywood? Put on a façade to help sell movies and records and a reputation?

Those blue eyes had inspired years' worth of girlish fantasies. What good was her bedroom poster now that she knew the truth?

"You have ruined him for me, Roan Bertoletti."

"Nah. He's still a great singer."

He'd made her laugh with his flippant tone, and the

memory wrapped around her like a butterfly's cocoon. She lifted both the Winchester and Rigby rifles from the gun rack for a swift dusting, then replaced them with care. And yet, even after they tidied the kitchen, took Mack for a long evening walk, and listened to the Jack Benny Radio Show, their differences remained an invisible wall between them.

She had to leave.

He was staying right here on the T Bar M Ranch.

And there came that heaviness in the pit of her stomach again. The same heaviness which robbed her of sleep and a solution. Rexanna had never been one to lose focus or flounder with indecision, but Roan threw her into uncharted territory, like a mountain that had never been climbed. A pinnacle which seemed impossible to reach.

Sighing, she went out to the porch and shook the dust off the flannel. Then, like she had all morning, she leaned around the edge of the cabin to study the road leading to the alpacas' pen.

Nothing.

Roan's pickup wasn't there. Again.

It was silly to keep hoping he'd come by to take care of the alpacas as a way to see her. She had no right to want him with her or to monopolize his time when his priorities were his ranch duties.

Something was happening, and she had an unsettling suspicion she knew what it was.

She re-entered the cabin, letting the screen door rattle shut behind her, and eyed the fake flowers on the mantel that had been sitting there for as long as she could remember. Dusty and faded and outdated, they had to go, and she set them on the floor for tossing in

the trash later. She could replace them with a framed picture, maybe. One of her hunting conquests, of which she'd documented many—
She halted the idea.
She was doing it again.
Thinking of the future. Here in Kansas, on this ranch, in this *cabin.*
She had to stop. *Stop.*
Her pulse fell into a rapid rhythm, her body turned feverish, and her gaze slid toward the mahogany box, still in its place. The only thing left on the mantel. The one object that claimed a legend and a mystery and a promise, all rolled into one.
The pink pistol.
Hands shaking, she took the gun case and set it on the blonde coffee table. Just so she could dust the mantel. Get it out of the way, of course, like anyone would.
But she didn't retrieve the flannel. She didn't resume her dusting. The mahogany case kept her staring, her heart pumping.
There must be something to it, this legend.
She stepped back from the coffee table, took a breath, and moved forward again. Bending, she lifted the lid on the case. Gingerly. She braced for the unexpected. Something different that would happen this time that hadn't happened before. A puff of smoke, maybe. Or a twisting, writhing fog that could reach up, cloud her vision, and stoke her imagination, painting a whimsy that might or might not be.
But nothing happened.
Nothing had changed.
There was only the small pistol with the pink

mother-of-pearl handle, still lying on the bed of green velvet. Smith & Wesson, .32 caliber, double action, like before. Even the folded parchment of Marriage Notes and the key and chain were there in the lining's pocket, right where she'd left them.

Rexanna eased out a breath.

Calmer, her stare fixed on the little weapon, her feet moving along the front of the coffee table. She took her time, waiting, gauging, like she would a herd of caribou during a hunt. She rounded the table, prepared for the slightest illusion, the faintest change. Her mind kept working, contemplating, wondering....

Had she gone crazy?

Was she no better than Aunt Trixie?

She couldn't believe the legend. She *couldn't*.

She strode full circle around the coffee table, and still, the pink pistol laid there. Unmoving. Silent. But she could feel its presence, as if it could stare up at her, waiting for its whimsy to take hold.

Rexanna refused to be like bait in a trap. She refused to wait until captured.

She scowled down at it. "You can't be doing this to me."

A ray of sunlight stretching through her clean windows sparkled on the mother-of-pearl handle. Mocking her. Defying her. Assuring her, oddly, it might listen.

"I can't fall in love with Roan Bertoletti. Do you hear me? I can't." She couldn't drag her eyes off the little gun. She couldn't break its pull. "I don't care what happened to all the other women who found husbands because of you. Good for them. Their Marriage Notes were lovely and romantic, but they happened *years* ago and have nothing to do with me."

She paced one side of the coffee table, and then the other. She stared down at it again.

"Look, it's just not going to work. I have to leave the ranch. I have a business to run. Maybe you don't know that, but I do."

Was she really having this conversation? Did the words need to be said to an inanimate object like a pink pistol?

How silly was that?

But she had to say them. She couldn't stop. She had to declare her stance out loud for her sake. For the legend's, too.

"Roan has found a home on the T Bar M. He's happy and fulfilled. He'll find another woman. He's handsome and strong. He's kind and compassionate and incredibly smart. He's every woman's dream. They'll fall at his feet in droves. He doesn't need me."

Her eyes stung. Her breath quickened. Her fists clenched.

She wasn't telling the pink pistol anything new. She'd had these same feelings in the middle of the night. The same logic.

Then why did it hurt so much to say so now?

"Why did you have to pick me, pink pistol? That's what you've done, isn't it? You've turned my heart onto Roan like no man before him. It's not fair." Her eyes narrowed. "But you messed up, you know that? I'm not the right woman for him. You need to find someone else to fall in love with him instead of me."

But what about her? When would she fall in love? Or with whom, if not with Roan?

She couldn't deny she missed having a man in her

life with a prospect of marriage and eventually a family with him, but she had few opportunities while on her hunting expeditions. Even Damien planned to marry someday and start his own family, and how could he raise one while traveling on hunting expeditions with her?

Rexanna covered her face with her hands.

It was all so confusing.

There was no solution, and she couldn't keep wasting time standing here and dwelling on the whole thing. Talking to a pink pistol, especially. She closed the mahogany lid with more noise than was necessary, scooped up the gun case, and stuffed it under the couch cushion.

There.

If she couldn't see it, she wouldn't think about it. And if she didn't think about it, her life would go on as before. Orderly and on schedule.

Logical.

Without the fake flowers or the mahogany case on its top, she finished dusting the mantel in a snap, then returned the flannel and Old English to their places under the sink. From another cupboard, she pulled out a plastic pitcher, filled it with water from the faucet, and headed outside.

She'd gotten the bedding plants on clearance at Perelman's Grocery store in a totally spontaneous buy, knowing they would liven the drab foundation with color, and she dribbled water on each one. They'd already perked up after transplanting, and even though she made sure each one got their share of water, it saddened her she wouldn't see them grow much longer.

Planting them had been a mistake.

13

"Sugar snap peas and green beans like to be planted in cool weather," Grandma said, straddling a lush row of the legumes. "Then, by the time they're ready to pick, the weather is just right. Not too cold, not too hot." She added a handful of slender beans to the growing pile in her bushel basket. "Your grandpa likes to eat the peas almost the moment they're picked. Just opens the pods and pops the peas into his mouth. They taste so fresh that way."

Rexanna worked the row next to her, albeit a bit

slower. "I remember doing that with him when I was little. He used to make me promise not to snitch that we were eating snap peas before you could can them. He always made sure to help himself when you weren't looking."

Laughing, her grandmother straightened. "He still does that, I'm afraid." Pressing a hand to the small of her back, she groaned dramatically. "Oh, bending over these bushes isn't as easy as it used to be."

Rexanna straightened, too, and frowned in concern. "Grandma, why don't you rest for a while? I can finish picking."

"Goodness, no, Rexi. Picking is the best part of gardening."

A gentle breeze plucked at the brim of her straw hat and lifted the hem of her housedress. Slender, with the faintest tan on her arms and face, she appeared relaxed and happy with her life and the chores that came along with it. Harrie Brennan was the epitome of a ranch wife, a vibrant part of the land among row after row of assorted vegetables. Her grandparents planted a large garden every spring, though admittedly, this one wasn't as large as some Rexanna remembered. But still plenty of work, with plentiful produce.

"You've always had a green thumb, haven't you?" Rexanna asked, delaying her picking to give her grandmother's back time to recuperate.

"From the time I was a young bride, I suppose." She smiled. "I was on my own then. My mother certainly wasn't going to do my gardening. I had to learn how, with her advice, of course."

"You make it look easy." Rexanna swept her arm outward. "Everything is healthy. The rows are full and perfectly spaced. You're going to have more green beans and sugar snap peas than you'll know what to do with. And they are only the beginning."

"We had a good spring. Some years, we aren't so lucky when the weather doesn't cooperate." She tugged on her hat brim, seeming to put off her bending a little longer. "Your dad had a green thumb, but he taught your mother how to garden. They loved working together. Then you came along, and as soon as you could walk, you'd toddle into the garden and pull out as many young seedlings as you could. You used to exasperate your mom and dad to no end."

They laughed at that, and Rexanna's spirits lifted as she took the memory of this time with her beloved grandmother into her heart.

"Would you like a garden of your own someday, Rexi?" Grandma asked quietly, her laughter fading.

Rexanna's did, too. She shrugged. "I don't think about it much." She glanced away, taking in the vast T Bar M range sprawling around them and very much aware of how her grandmother studied her, as if Rexanna's response mattered. A lot. "Can't grow things when you're not around, right?"

Like petunias around a foundation. Or a lawn that needed tending. Or alpacas that needed caring for... and yes, a garden, too.

"Surely, you think of having a home of your own?" Grandma asked gently. "A husband? Babies? Eventually?"

Rexanna's eyes smarted. She couldn't speak, lest she choke on the words.

"Well."

She braced at her grandmother's tone of voice. She

had an opinion coming, and Rexanna knew to just let her have at it. A lifetime of respect for the Brennan matriarch allowed for nothing else, and Rexanna wouldn't be the first in the family to be its target.

"It seems to me, Rexi, you're of a prime age for all those things. You can't be hunting wild game all the time. It's a hard life. An unsettled one. It's dangerous, too." She didn't need to mention Annie's name to make Rexanna know that Annie was on her mind. "You need to think about putting down roots. Do you suppose there's a bear or a mountain lion or—or a moose or whatever else you hunt who cares one whit about you? Then why should you care so much about them?"

Rexanna forced a tight smile. "I don't believe anyone has spoken of my outfitting business quite that way before, Grandma."

Her grandmother reached across the row of green beans and gently tucked strands of hair behind Rexanna's ear. But her expression showed no apology.

"We're very proud of what you've accomplished. Very few women have done what you have. But there are people on this ranch who care more for you than you realize. We worry about you constantly, Rexi. Weeks, months go by, and we don't even know where you are."

"I'm sorry." She bit her lip. It was true, and if the situation were reversed, Rexanna would worry, too. "But wild game hunting is what I do. It's something I enjoy, and—and I'm good at it. It's all I really know, hunting."

"Cord was a bounty hunter when I met him." Her features softened. "He was good at it, too. The best around at the time. But his father was a cripple, and

Cord was prepared to give up chasing outlaws to take care of him. And then he met me, and he took up cattle ranching, instead." She smiled, the memory clearly a fond one. "Trace, your great-grandfather, was a bounty hunter—"

"Grandma, I know." Rexanna held up her hand. "I've heard all this before. You've made your point."

"Forgive me if I'm putting too much pressure on you, but I needed to get it off my chest. My point being that people can make changes, and their lives are better for it. Oh, Rexi." Grandma's voice quivered. "When you leave, your grandfather and I will wonder if it'll be the last time we see you." Her eyes welled, and Rexanna's heart twisted. Rarely did she see her grandmother show tears. Had she ever, except when Rexanna's parents were killed? "That's not an easy thing for us. You're all we have left."

Rexanna's control crumpled, and she covered her face with her hands. She didn't want to be the reason for her grandmother's tears. She hated hearing Grandma's gut-wrenching admission for wanting Rexanna to stay, this baring of her soul at the possibility of losing the youngest member of her family.

Before Rexanna could wrestle her anguish into submission, her grandmother pulled her against her bosom, the bushes of green beans between them at their feet, and held her tight.

"You're always so strong, Rexi. I've not seen you this troubled." Grandma rubbed her back, over and over again. "Don't you want to leave?"

"I don't know what to do. I've loved being here with you. And, oh, Roan... he's made everything so much more... special." She hiccupped and drew back. "He told me the same thing you're telling me now. Have you two been hatching a plot to keep me on the ranch?"

Her grandmother emitted a surprised laugh. "Did he? No, I haven't spoken to him about you at all. His words are his own. I promise."

"He keeps telling me about the ranch. My responsibilities here."

"He doesn't want you to leave, either."

Her shoulders slumped. "No. I don't think so."

"I think maybe you've caught his eye."

"As in?"

"Fallen in love with you."

"That's just silly." But the pink pistol flared in her memory, its mother-of-pearl handle sparkling in the living room light. "*Silly*, Grandma."

Grandma exhaled. "The decision will always be yours. But Roan is a fine man. A wonderful cowboy. He's become a valued part of the T Bar M." She hesitated. "Just so you know."

Rexanna stared. What did *that* mean?

The crazy notion that he might take her place on the T Bar M reared in her head like a kicking, wild horse. Would her grandparents allow that? When he wasn't even a Brennan?

Could Rexanna allow that to happen? Her inheritance? Her birthright?

Or would she be much too selfish in wanting to keep both worlds for herself... her outfitting business and her family's ranch?

But she couldn't have both.

It would be impossible.

Grandma stepped back, taking care not to crush growing bean plants. "Talk to your partner, Damien. Maybe you two can come up with a solution."

She pouted. "What kind of a solution?"

"A compromise." She lifted her bushel basket and moved it farther down the row. "You'll figure it out, Rexi. But you'll have to hurry." Bending, she picked another handful of snap peas. "My basket is filling up. Would you like to help me can beans this afternoon?"

Several hours later, Rexanna pulled up in front of the cabin and cut the Ford's ignition. After she exited the driver's seat, taking her purse with her, she let Mack out the passenger side, and both of them tromped up the porch stairs.

Holding the screen door with her hip, she no sooner slid the door key into the lock when the phone pealed. With a flick of her wrist, the door swung open, and she hurried inside to answer.

Roan parked the ranch pickup behind Rexanna's in the drive and got out. He half-expected to find Mack on his rope in the front yard, but the coonhound wasn't out. Strange, since it was a nice afternoon, one he'd enjoy taking a snooze in.

Roan climbed the stairs, dipping his head as always to avoid Trixie's little birdies. The front door was open, giving him full access to see into the living room and kitchen, but neither Rexanna nor Mack were visible. Roan's knock sounded loud in the cabin's quiet, and while he waited, he checked the soles of his boots, one after the other. No mud or manure to warrant any scolding. Bits of hay clung to his Levi's, though, and he brushed them off. Rexanna wouldn't appreciate those on her clean floors, either.

"Rexanna."

Like his knock, his call to her sounded loud but went unanswered, too, and after a few more moments, he opened the screen door and went inside. There'd be a logical reason why she wasn't around, but it was strange he couldn't smell food cooking. It was getting to be suppertime, and she liked to keep a schedule. His whole purpose in stopping by hinged on an invitation to join her.

One of the couch cushions lay cockeyed next to the other, and that was odd, too. Rexanna preferred a neat house, and he couldn't imagine how she might have missed the disheveled cushion, or even tolerated it, but he leaned over to right it. The mahogany case beneath threw him, and why she'd put it *there* only added more oddness to the growing pile of oddities coming at him.

Grasping the wooden box in one hand, he re-settled the cushion with the other. He lifted the lid for a quick check. The pink pistol was there, like it should be, which only made her hiding the thing more puzzling.

She didn't want to see it.

He frowned.

After putting the gun case back on the mantel, he headed toward the kitchen. Her bedroom door stood open, her bed neatly made, as usual, but it was the suitcase on top, filled with clothes, that chilled him clear to his bones.

Footsteps scuffed outside, and he spun toward the sound. The back door swung wide, and Mack trotted in. Rexanna followed, wrangling a basket of towels through the opening. Seeing him, she froze with a little gasp.

"Hello, Rexanna," he said, his voice more of a growl than a greeting.

Her throat worked. "Roan."

"I knocked," he said roughly. "You didn't answer."

"I was taking towels off the line."

"I see that."

Slowly, letting the door bang shut behind her, she set the basket down. Mack rubbed against his thigh. Roan ignored him.

"Going somewhere?" he asked, still not moving. Still barely breathing.

"Yes." She took a step toward him, but only one. "I have to go back to Alaska."

"Alaska." He eyed her, as if she could disappear right into thin air. Which, in truth, she would. Apparently. "When?"

"As soon as I finish up around here."

His fists clenched. It was all he could do to keep standing there, talking to her. To breathe and think and try to understand.

"I have to be in California in the morning," she added. "I'll drive all night, for as long as I can, at least."

"You know how dangerous that is? How tired you'll be?"

"I'll find a motel along the way, if I have to." She hesitated. "I've done it before."

The worry swarmed through him, hot and fierce, and she hadn't even left the cabin yet.

"I was going to ride out to tell you as soon as I was," she said in a rush. "Finished, I mean."

"Glad you could give me at least that."

"Don't, Roan. Please."

"Don't, Roan, what?" he demanded. "Don't be blindsided by any of this? Don't be hoping you'll stay on the ranch? Don't want you leaving again? Ever?"

Her chin quivered. "I have to."

"Why?"

She inhaled. Exhaled. "Damien called this afternoon. Stuart and Patrice Langford, Annie's parents, are building a memorial for her on the mountain where she was killed. They've gotten permission... they want me there... because... I was her guide and everything."

"Send Damien instead."

"I can't." She swallowed. "He's been in Africa, taking my place so I could come here for Aunt Trixie's funeral. He gave me the time off, but in Tanzania, he contracted malaria, and now, he's too sick to go to Alaska, and I didn't know any of this until he called."

Roan swore inwardly. Could things get any worse?

"He'll be transferred to a hospital here in the States in a day or two, he said. He's improved that much, at least, but he won't be able to hunt anytime soon."

"So that leaves you."

She nodded, the movement jerky. "Just me."

"And after that? After the memorial service."

She tucked her hair behind her ear, and a desire, a *need*, resurrected within him to spear his hands into that mane of hers and breathe in its scent. To just bury his face into the thickness and lock the memory inside him.

"I have another excursion lined up. Bear again. Same mountain."

His teeth gritted. "When will it end, Rexanna?"

Looking miserable, she shrugged a slender shoulder. "We're booked... a ways out."

"Of course, you would be."

Her glance shot back toward him. "It's my business, Roan. I've worked a long time to be successful."

"I know."

"But...." Her voice trailed off, and she stared at her toes.

Her unhappiness pulled at him. He couldn't keep from moving toward her and taking her into his arms any more than he could save himself after falling over a cliff.

She sank against him, curling her arms around his waist, and hanging on like her life had gone sideways.

Because maybe it did. Like his.

"But what, Rexi?" he murmured, his jaw against her hair.

"I've never not wanted to leave like I don't want to leave now."

"Yeah?" His mouth curved. He felt her pout more than he could see it.

Maybe there was hope, after all.

She drew her head back, and her red-brown eyes shot little sparks of fire up at him.

"I've always loved the traveling, but now I'm dreading it, and it's your fault, Roan. Yours and Grandma's and the pink pistol's. All of you came at me with your barrels locked and loaded, and I didn't have a chance to fight back against any of you."

She looked so serious, he had to work hard to keep from laughing, so great were the crazy emotions soaring through him.

"I love you, Rexanna," he murmured, cupping the side of her face with his palm.

Her lips moved downward. "I love you, too, Roan. I don't want to, but it's happened, and I don't quite know what to do about it."

His head lowered, and he captured her mouth with his. Long, slow, and lingering, with as much love as he could pour into it.

"I'll wait for you," he whispered before kissing her again. "For as long as it takes."

She burrowed closer, her embrace tighter. "I can't ask that of you. I don't know how long I'll be... I have commitments..."

"Doesn't matter. The T Bar M is my home. I'll be here until you're ready to make it yours, too."

Later, when the drive stood empty except for his ranch pickup, after Rexanna made her goodbyes to her grandparents, Roan hung back to close up the cabin. He turned off the lights, made sure the back door was locked, and just as he would've exited through the front to lock that one, too, something indefinable compelled him to pause on the threshold and turn around.

The pink pistol graced the mantel in unassuming silence, its promise shielded within the green velvet lining and aged mahogany. The memory of Rexanna's kisses and the feel of her against him warmed his blood and lived in his heart, a gift that filled his future with promise.

Maybe there was something to the legend, after all.

Later That Fall

Rexanna scraped the sides of the mixing bowl and mounded the last of the cookie dough onto the sheet, then opened the oven door and exchanged baked cookies for unbaked ones. After setting the hot sheet aside to cool, she removed her oven mitt, set the timer, and headed to the sink to wash both the bowl and beater.

The high-end, late-model mixer had been one of

her grandmother's wedding gifts to her, and she'd given it with the sage advice that husbands and children should be spoiled with all the good food a good mixer could help prepare. She assured Rexanna that, even with a houseful of little Bertoletti children to feed, the mixer would keep on mixing, time after time.

A smart woman, her grandmother.

As Rexanna prepared to rinse the suds off the glass bowl, the light streaming in from the kitchen window caught on her wedding ring. Soapy bubbles and water enhanced the sparkling diamonds on her wedding and engagement set.

Seeing them never failed to move her, and she pressed her lips to the solitaire, watery suds and all. Even now, she could hardly believe she'd wear the rings on her finger forever. Roan had been generous in his choice, and her surprise had been unmatched. Never had she owned anything so beautiful.

But then, never had she loved a man like Roan, either.

Five days ago, they married. With her grandmother's help, Rexanna pulled the wedding together as soon as she returned to the ranch after her last hunting excursion. The Chevrolet's engine barely had time to cool before she jumped into a whirlwind of details, organizing, cooking, even finding time to shop in Kansas City for the wedding dress of her dreams....

After a simple ceremony in the church, her grandparents had invited the entire Wallace community and a whole slew of area ranchers for a barbecue fit for a king and with enough food to feed an army. A honeymoon would wait, perhaps to a warmer destination in the midst of the sometimes-brutal Kansas winter. Rexanna was in no hurry to leave the T Bar M. After years of being gone, she much preferred instead to start her new life with Roan right here on the ranch.

By the time she rinsed and dried the bowl, beater, and returned the mixer to its place on the counter, the gumdrop cookies were done. Leaving the entire batch to cool on paper before she added them to the cookie jar, she gathered a half dozen onto a plate, took a pair of glasses from the cupboard, added ice, and poured cold tea over them. Taking all three, balancing them carefully, she headed out the kitchen and onto the porch.

It'd become a habit for Roan to stop by the house to see her in the afternoon, if he could. She always had something ready for him, whether a hot drink or a cold one, a snack or two, and if his choice leaned more toward her and less on food, well, she gave him that, as well.

Had she ever been happier?

As much as she loved wild game hunting, she loved being Roan's wife more. Two loves couldn't be more different, but each was fulfilling in its own way. Her life was richer for both.

After setting the cookies and iced tea on the simple wooden table he'd built in front of the new porch swing, she descended the steps and searched for him as she often did when she was outside. Not surprising, she found him with the alpacas. When he wasn't tending cattle, he was tending them, and while she was gone, he'd tripled the size of the herd, which required a bigger pen. He'd built that, too, with her grandfather's help, and the long-necked creatures moved freely among one another.

Little camel lookalikes, and they never failed to make her smile.

Woo-hoo-hoo.

Mack caught sight of her, and his howl caught Roan's attention, too. She waved, but her dog didn't come running. He'd become Roan's as much as hers now, but that was fine with her. The three of them, a family.

Roan tousled the coonhound's head and said something, and Mack took off in his usual graceful lope toward her. He practically skidded to a stop upon reaching her, making her laugh, and she lavished him with plenty of chin rubs.

"You sweet boy. Want to sit on the porch with me? I have treats."

Tail wagging, he bounded up the stairs and waited, his attention on her focused and expectant, but Rexanna hung back to watch Roan's approach.

His Stetson shadowed his Mediterranean dark looks and the strong planes of his face. Warmth spread through her blood. She knew his body now, as intimately as her own, from the corded muscles on his shoulders, to his flat belly, to the appealing taper of his hips. He walked with a quiet grace and subdued power, pure cowboy and man, and she had to pinch herself to know for sure it was all real.

That he was completely hers.

Of their own accord, her feet moved toward him, and he took her into his arms, giving her a long squeeze, so tight against him his belt buckle pressed into her abdomen. She leaned her head back, and he dropped a lazy kiss onto her mouth.

"I have cookies," she said softly.

"Gumdrop, I hope." His smile revealed his tease.

"Just for you, cowboy."

"Let me have at 'em."

He hooked an arm around her shoulders, and they fell into a comfortable stroll toward the house. No longer Aunt Trixie's cabin, but their home now. Their stake into the future. Their part of the T Bar M on the section of land her grandparents had gifted them for their wedding.

The Bertoletti homestead.

The petunias had flourished throughout the summer—what little she'd seen of them—thanks to Grandma's and Roan's watering, but the ground had been cleared for the winter, and she missed their color.

"After the house is painted, we could add some bushes along the foundation." She voiced her thoughts aloud. "Dogwood, maybe. Or an evergreen of some sort. I could border them with an assortment of flowers."

"You'll have to decide on a house color first. Can't paint until you do."

"A cypress green, I think, with white trim all around."

"That'll look nice, yeah."

She tilted her glance up toward him. "The green will remind me of trees on the mountains."

"You'll have all the green you want right here on the ranch, too."

"True." Her mouth softened. "A different kind of green, but just as beautiful."

Overhead, a skein of ducks flew in V formation. Their honking drew Mack off the porch with a bounding leap into the yard, until he seemed to remember where he was. He stopped abruptly with his nose lifted into the air, his body taut.

"You think he'll miss his old life?" Roan asked quietly.

"He's happy here, in his new one," she said, convinced of it, given all the attention Roan lavished him. "It's not like he'll never hunt again."

"Just smaller game."

"And closer to home. He likes the comforts of living in a warm house now, instead of a tent somewhere in the cold wilderness."

Roan turned, tucking her hair behind her ear like he often did. "How about you, Rexi? Will you miss your old life after you tire of living your new one with me?"

His dark brows connected, and his expression shadowed, tearing at her insides. A rare thing to see Roan Bertoletti unsure of himself. She faced him, sliding her arms around his lean waist.

"I'd be lying if I said I wouldn't miss it," she said in quiet honesty. "Hunting wild game is all I've ever done, but I can't do it forever. I don't *want* to do it forever."

"Hunting season is beginning around here. Those ducks are only the start."

"I'll hunt as long as I can carry a rifle, but on my terms. Not someone else's." She leaned upward and kissed him, fervently enough to let him know she meant every word. Flooded with the memories of how circumstances she never expected to happen helped her make the decision she needed to make, she drew back. "When I returned to California, and Stuart Langford mentioned he had a friend looking to expand his outfitting business, it was a gift from God. An opportunity that landed in my lap, one that I couldn't pass up. Not once have I regretted my decision to sell my business, Roan."

By the time the details had been finalized, Damien was feeling strong enough to join her. When the new owner needed to expand his roster of guides, giving Damien the job, well, that was a gift from God, too.

"Hard to travel when we have cattle to take care of," he murmured.

"Hard to make babies when I'm not here with you."

"Babies?" His brow shot up, and his worry vanished, like buckshot in the wind. "Well, hey. Let's go inside, and we can take care of that right now."

She laughed and held up a hand. "Not yet. I have cookies, remember?"

"Oh, yeah."

Chuckling, he took her hand and led her up the porch stairs, letting her precede him before he sat on the porch swing. He didn't even have to dip his head these days, not since he donated Aunt Trixie's hanging things to his friend with the art exhibit place. Rexanna had kept one for herself in her aunt's memory, and it hung proudly in the corner of their bedroom.

But she wasn't ready to sit on the swing just yet.

"There's something I need to do, Roan," she said, handing him a glass of iced tea and the plate of gumdrop cookies. "I'll be right back."

Inside the house, she headed straight for the mantel. The mahogany gun case seemed to wait for what needed to be done. The recording of a promise fulfilled.

She took a pen and the gun case, then headed back

to the porch. Mack sat at Roan's feet, expecting a bite of cookie. Rexanna stepped around him, and the swing took her weight. Sitting hip to hip with Roan, she lifted the lid.

The pink pistol glimmered among the green velvet, pretty as always. Rexanna removed the folded parchment from the lining's pocket, carefully unfolded it, and re-read the pistol's letter.

"... *She who possesses this pistol, possesses an opportunity that must not be squandered.*"

"Can't say as you've squandered an opportunity," Roan said in his low voice, reading with her. "You married me, right?" He kissed the top of her head. "Smart girl."

"... *the steel of this weapon is steadfast and true and will lead an unmarried woman to a man forged from the same virtuous elements.*"

"And you are certainly steadfast and true," she said, snuggling closer. "I'm not only smart, but I'm blessed, too, with your virtuousness."

"... *open her heart to activate the promise*..."

Her eyes filled at the words. "I opened my heart to you, Roan Bertoletti, and you fell right in."

"Where I intend to stay, for as long as you'll have me."

"... *until her heart finds its home.*"

"I'll have you forever, Roan. Because my heart is joined with yours." She blinked fast. "Now, before I start crying all over this century-old parchment, I have to write our Marriage Note."

"You know what you're going to say?"

"I've been thinking on it for days."

Her gaze lingered over the last written inscription:

Mariah Bartee finally succumbed to Dax Talon's charms and married him on the first day of spring, March 20, 1940. She traded security and love for the danger and secrets she'd known for most of her life. It was a peaceful new beginning for both.

1940. Now, here it was, 1955, and it was Rexanna's turn. She began to write....

Rexanna Brennan married Roan Bertoletti on September 29, 1955. I've shot exotic game worthy of the finest of trophies, but my cowboy's love has been my biggest prize of all.

Rexanna sighed, still caught in the emotion swirling through her heart. Setting the pen aside, she gently refolded the parchment and returned it to the lining pocket with the case's key and chain nestled inside.

Now that she'd found her happiness with Roan, she had no further use for the pink pistol. But one day, some other woman would. Until that time came, Rexanna would guard it as fiercely as the love she'd found.

Annie Oakley would be proud.

THE END

LUCKY SHOT

BY SHANNA HATFIELD

Boise, Idaho
May 1972

Ribbons of sunshine gliding through the leaves of the trees around her caressed Grace Marshall's cheek. Eyes closed, she tipped her head back to accept the gift of warmth and breathed deeply of the fresh air.

Thankfully, no one else was currently in the place used by the Boise Veterans Administration Hospital nurses as a break area when the weather was pleasant. Without the scent of cigarette smoke filling the air and the peaceful quiet of a spring day surrounding her, it was easy for Grace to block from her mind the challenging morning she'd endured, assisting an egotistical doctor with two impossible patients.

Grace turned on the transistor radio on the table, where she sat and listened as Otis Redding sang about sitting on the dock of a bay. She could sure use a vacation. What would it be like to head south, somewhere that already felt like summer, and dangle her feet in the water? Maybe spend an entire afternoon doing nothing but bathing in the sun and indulging in fruity drinks.

Then again, she could always head home to Holiday and sit with her feet in the water of one of the lovely lakes in the area. Her mom had a great strawberry lemonade recipe, and there was the pineapple punch she'd made for a birthday party last August that everyone still talked about.

Just thinking about her family in the Eastern Oregon community where she'd grown up made her lonesome to see her parents and brothers. Only Micah remained at home, though, helping with their dairy farm. Jared was with the Marines in Vietnam, although Grace had no idea of his current location. Jason was off at college in Corvallis, finishing his third year of working toward a degree in agribusiness.

As Grace bit into the roast beef sandwich loaded with pickles and celery her roommate had made for her that morning, she thought about how much she missed her mom's cheeseburger pie and chicken casserole. Grace had the recipes and could make them, but they never tasted quite the same.

She shook her head, attempting to dislodge her homesickness. She'd lived in Boise for three years, but there were still moments she longed to be back in Holiday, where the air smelled like Christmas and most everyone seemed like family.

In Boise, Grace often felt lost in the crowd, but she

was finding her way and, she hoped, making life a little better for the patients she helped at the VA Hospital.

She glanced at the assortment of magazines on the table. Elizabeth Taylor and her grandson graced the cover of *Ladies' Home Journal*, along with promises for sew-and-go fashions that could be made in a day, if one had time for sewing. She glanced at an article about an opportunity to win a free vacation.

"Not likely," she muttered, took another bite of the sandwich, then picked up the latest copy of *McCall's* magazine. It offered nostalgic needlework ideas and had one of her favorite features—a bonus historical romance story. Grace loved to read; she just didn't get much time to enjoy it.

Quickly opening the magazine to the story, she was soon engrossed in the tale. It wasn't until she heard a chair squeak that she realized she was no longer alone.

"Hey, Susie. How are things going for you today?" she asked as she dabbed her mouth with a paper napkin, then took a drink of the Coca-Cola she'd purchased from the vending machine inside. Little droplets of condensation slid along the neck of the glass bottle as she tilted it to her lips.

"As good as can be," Susie said, reaching for the *Cosmopolitan* magazine and flipping it open before she folded back the waxed paper on her cheese sandwich and took a bite.

Grace returned to the story and her lunch, enjoying both before she glanced at the watch on her wrist and knew it was time to head back inside. How she wished she could yank off the white stockings she wore and bask in the sunshine this afternoon. Instead, she had plenty of patients to see and important work to do.

"See you later," she said to Susie, then gathered her things and returned inside.

An hour into her afternoon shift, she wished she'd stayed outside. One cranky patient had yelled at her when she'd tried to check his pulse, and one downright nasty man had threatened her just as the doctor walked in. Thankfully, Dr. O'Brien had asked her to send in one of the older nurses to deal with the unpleasant patient.

By the time her work wrapped up for the day, Grace was exhausted and more than ready to head back to the apartment she shared with her best friend.

She and Cindy Milton had been friends since they were old enough to walk. They were in the same grade in school and even had crushes on the same boy in their junior year of high school. However, Caleb had returned Cindy's affection. The two of them had been engaged to marry before he'd gotten himself killed in Vietnam.

Thoughts of the war always made Grace's heart feel as heavy as one of the anvils Cindy's grandfather kept in the old livery building in Holiday. She hated that so many young men had died. Almost as tragic was the way the returning soldiers were treated by so many, as though they had single-handedly caused the war. Political views aside, Grace thought anyone who fought for America deserved respect and gratitude.

She knew how hard it was on soldiers to go off to war, and not just from the men she treated at the hospital. Her father as well as her Uncle Thad had fought in World War II. While her father had survived his time spent in the Pacific battling the Japanese, Uncle Thad had been killed by a German bullet in France, leaving behind a wife and two children who missed him still. Although her father rarely talked about the war, Grace knew he still occasionally had nightmares that would wake them all in the stillness of the night.

The dark thoughts circling like vultures in her mind weren't appropriate for such a lovely day. When her shift ended, Grace stepped out into the bright spring sunshine and shrugged them away.

"Do you and Cindy have plans this evening?" Susie asked, falling into step with Grace as they walked across the lot where the staff parked.

"No. At least none of which I'm aware," Grace said with a grin. Cindy, who was full of fun, often talked her into spur-of-the-moment adventures.

"Well, after a busy day like today, on our feet at the beck and call of the doctors, I think we deserve a quiet evening to rest." Susie sighed as she set her purse inside her car and unpinned the hat from her short hair. "However, I have no doubt my husband will expect dinner on the table as usual."

"I hope you have a nice evening. See you tomorrow." Grace waved at Susie, then continued walking to her car, a hand-me-down from her oldest brother. Micah had bought the sporty two-door Chevrolet Impala brand new out of a showroom six years ago, but last fall, he'd purchased a new pickup and asked Grace if she'd like to have the car, no strings attached. She'd practically screamed in his ear when he'd phoned to offer the car to her. She'd loved it the moment Micah had driven it home, and she loved it even more now that it was hers.

Although the weather hadn't offered too many days warm enough to roll down the windows and let the wind blow through her hair, Grace looked forward to it this summer.

Like Susie, she unpinned the hat from her head and loosened the top two buttons of her uniform as she waited for Cindy.

Cindy didn't like to drive or own a vehicle and preferred it that way. Typically, though, her friend beat her to the car. Rather than linger in concern over why Cindy was late, Grace reached behind the seat and retrieved a paper tablet, scrounged a pen out of her purse, then started writing a letter to send to Jared.

It had been a while since she'd written to him. If she hurried, she could bake a batch of brown sugar drops tonight, then get a care package ready to mail to him tomorrow. She'd collected a few things she thought he might enjoy, like a new book Jason had recommended, and packages of Jared's favorite gum and candy. Jared loved Fruit Stripe gum and was the only one in their family who preferred Butter Rum Life Savers to any other flavor. Just for fun, she planned to include some Pixy Stix and a few boxes of Lemonhead candy.

Attention centered on the letter she wrote, describing the weather, the wall she and Cindy had painted in their apartment's bathroom, and family news he might not have heard, she sucked in a gasp when her friend yanked open the car door and plopped onto the passenger seat.

"Man, I am beat. Let's go home." Cindy set her purse between her feet and looked over at Grace. "You look awful." Her nose wrinkled. "And what is on your uniform?"

Grace glanced down at the stains on her dress and shook her head. "You don't want to know."

"You're right. I don't."

Grace ripped from the tablet the pages she'd written on and tucked them into her purse, then started the car. "Any side trips on the way home?"

"Not tonight." Cindy rolled down her window and rested her elbow on the door, drawing in a deep breath as she visibly relaxed. "Gosh, it was a long day, wasn't it?"

"No argument from me." Grace wondered what had happened to make her sunshiny friend look more like a raincloud. Cindy worked in the administrative offices at the hospital, but most often, she ended her workday with the same chipper attitude with which it began.

Grace might have found it highly annoying if she hadn't loved her friend so much. Cindy had always been sweet and cheerful. Even after losing her fiancé, she'd managed to offer comfort to those around her while she had stoically worked her way through her grief.

Two years later, Cindy remained alone and unattached, and Grace worried she might never date again, but if time truly healed all wounds, then perhaps love awaited Cindy somewhere in the future.

Love had proven to be quite an elusive thing, at least where Grace was concerned. Then again, she'd never been deeply in love with anyone. Not the way Cindy had loved and been loved. Grace longed to have that kind of soul connection with another and often dreamed of the day she might have a husband and family of her own. She was so busy with work and everything else in her life she didn't have much time or energy left for dating, even if she'd met someone who sparked her interest. Which she hadn't. Not yet. But a girl couldn't give up hoping to find true love.

Love this excerpt of LUCKY SHOT by Shanna Hatfield and want to read more?

Order on Amazon! https://amzn.to/3oN96oU

Books in the Pink Pistol Sisterhood Series

In Her Sights by **Karen Witemeyer**
Book 1 ~ March 30

Love on Target by **Shanna Hatfield**
Book 2 ~ April 10

Love Under Fire by **Cheryl Pierson**
Book 3 ~ April 20

Bulletproof Bride by **Kit Morgan**
Book 4 ~ April 30

Bullseye Bride by **Kari Trumbo**
Book 5 ~ May 10

Disarming His Heart by **Winnie Griggs**
Book 6 ~ May 20

One Shot at Love by **Linda Broday**
Book 7 ~ May 30

Armed & Marvelous by **Pam Crooks**
Book 8 ~ June 10

Lucky Shot **by Shanna Hatfield**
Book 9 ~~~ June 20

Aiming for His Heart **by Julie Benson**
Book 10 ~~~ June 30

Pistol Perfect **by Jessie Gussman**
Book 11 ~~~ July 10

See all the Pink Pistol Sisterhood Books on the Amazon Series Page: https://amzn.to/3SE1DDD

About Pam

While expecting her first child (more years back than she cares to count), Pam Crooks read her very first romance novel, and she's been in love with them ever since. She grew up in the ranch country of western Nebraska, and it was inevitable she'd eventually write lots of books about cowboys. Pam still lives in Nebraska with her husband (who is not a cowboy), four married daughters and a whole slew of perfect grandchildren.

Pam is also one of the founders of Petticoats & Pistols, a popular blogsite for western romance. She loves to cook, hang out at her lake cabin, and decorate birthday cakes for anyone who will let her.

To see other books Pam has written, visit www.pamcrooks.com and sign up for her newsletter!

Follow her on:
Bookbub -
https://www.bookbub.com/authors/pam-crooks
Facebook – www.facebook.com/pamcrooks

More by Pam Crooks

Sweet Historical Romances
Armed & Marvelous
Christiana
Harriett
Trace
Eleanora

Sweet Contemporary Romances
The Blackstone Ranch Series
A Cowboy and a Promise
Her Texas Cowboy
Her Kind of Cowboy

Single-Title Historicals
The Mercenaries Series
The Mercenary's Kiss
Her Lone Protector

C Bar C Ranch Series
Untamed Cowboy
Kidnapped by the Cowboy

Wells Cattle Company Series
The Cattleman's Unsuitable Wife
The Cattleman's Christmas Bride
The Lawman's Redemption

Broken Blossoms
Hannah's Vow
Lady Gypsy
Wyoming Wildflower

Boxed Set
In the Arms of a Cowboy

Christmas Novellas
The Christmas Rose
The Cattleman's Christmas Bride
One Magic Eve

Contemporary Romantic Suspense
Her Mother's Killer

Historical Romantic Suspense
The Secret Six Series
The Spyglass Project
In the Enemy's Shadow
The Brewer's Daughter

Made in the USA
Middletown, DE
03 September 2023